LET'S PLAY WHITE

APEX PUBLICATIONS
LEXINGTON, KY

Let's Play White

Copyright © 2011 Chesya Burke
Cover art © 2011 Jordan Casteel
Cover design by Justin Stewart
Interior design by Jason Sizemore

"Purse" © 2004, *Tales from the Gorezone*; "Chocolate Park" © 2004, Undaunted Press; "He Who Takes Away the Pain" © 2004, *Dark Dreams*; "The Room Where Ben Disappeared" © 2005, *Would That It Were*; "The Light of Cree" © 2006, *Voices from the Other Side*; "The Unremembered" © 2010, *Dark Faith* (Apex Publications). "Walter and the Three-Legged King", "I Make People Do Bad Things", "What She Saw When They Flew Away", "CUE: Change", and "The Teachings and Redemption of Ms. Fannie Lou Mason" are original to this edition.

Published by Apex Publications, LLC
PO Box 24323
Lexington, KY 40524

www.apexbookcompany.com

First Edition: May 2011

ISBN PB: 978-1-937009-99-1

For Shadvina Leavell and all those who were lost but never forgotten.

—Table of Contents—

We Wear the Mask

We wear the mask that grins and lies,
It hides our cheeks and shades our eyes,—
This debt we pay to human guile;
With torn and bleeding hearts we smile,
And mouth with myriad subtleties.

Why should the world be over-wise,
In counting all our tears and sighs?
Nay, let them only see us, while
    We wear the mask.

We smile, but, O great Christ, our cries
To thee from tortured souls arise.
We sing, but oh the clay is vile
Beneath our feet, and long the mile;
But let the world dream otherwise,
    We wear the mask!

—Paul Laurence Dunbar, *Lyrics of Lowly Life*, 1896

"WALTER AND THE THREE-LEGGED KING"

S hit droppings on the sink were always evidence that the rat had been there. Walter hated the beast; it did nothing but live off the crumbs he left. It survived—it *thrived*—off of his misery. Day after day he watched the thing grow fat while he wasted away. Walter wondered if he died right there on the floor, if the rat would eat his rotting corpse. That was okay. As soon as he got the chance, Walter was gonna catch the thing and choke the shit outta it with his bare hands. And if that didn't work, then he would figure something out. One way or another, he would defeat that rat.

Walter searched the counters, fixing his shirt into the waistline of his pants. The damn thing had gotten into the pots that he'd made last night's stew in, licking the remaining sauce from the cheap steel. *Damn it.* He needed to start washing everything, including the counters and all, the night he used it. That should help. At least it would keep the damn thing off his counters. Then maybe it would go and bother one of his neighbors in that godforsaken building.

As Walter turned to walk back into the room for his shoes, the rat stared at him from a small hole where the wall met the floor. Why hadn't he noticed that gap before? The rat was completely still. It stood on its hind legs, its ears perked up, listening. After a moment, it ventured out farther into the living room, keeping its eyes on Walter. Jesus, the thing was bold.

Walter moved slowly, trying not to make any sudden motions. Here was his chance. He could put an end to this right now. The man turned back to the sink, slowly, keeping an eye on the filthy little beast, and grabbed the closest thing he could reach. He wrapped his hands around the dirty stew pot from the night before, aimed, then threw it toward the rat. The pot sailed through the air, picking up speed, as the handle twirled clumsily, over and over in a circle. Just as the pot hit the floor, Walter knew he was off. By only a few inches, but enough for it to matter. The rat jumped at the sound, ran around in a circle, and then ducked back into the hole. The pot bounced off the floor, hit the walls, and splashed leftover not-quite-stew all over the apartment.

Walter looked at the mess, then at his imitation Rolex wrist watch. He'd gotten it off a street vender for the low, low price of five bucks. It didn't particularly look like a Rolex, and it didn't keep the time all that well, but what the hell, it had been cheap. Either way, the watch wasn't completely wrong; right now he didn't have the time to clean up the mess. He had an interview in less than forty-five minutes. Well. He guessed there would be no need for the rat to climb the counters now—as long as Walter was willing to throw food right at it, this rat would eat like a king.

He had barely made it back into the apartment again before the landlord came rapping at the door. Walter didn't have to guess who it was; nobody else bothered to visit him. Jerry wouldn't either if Walter didn't owe him money. He stood, stepped over the mess that he still hadn't bothered to clean up, and opened the door. Jerry stood there, gnawing on a turkey leg the size of Walter's calf.

"'Sup, Walter." As he spoke, food spilled onto his shirt, the blue veins in his white cheeks swelling with every chew.

"Nothin' much." Walter didn't invite him in, and he wasn't gonna. As long as his name was on the lease and he still had possession, he would reserve that right. Though the way things looked, that wouldn't be too much longer. All the more reason to keep the man standing at the door.

"So, how's everything, man?"

"It is what it is."

"Oh?" Jerry was notorious for beating around the bush.

"Yep." Walter's belly began to rumble. As disgusting as it looked, that turkey leg smelled delicious. All he had in his icebox was leftover meatless stew. He wasn't even sure that stew could be called stew if it had no meat.

"Look, Walter, did you get the job, man?"

Walter looked him square in the eye. He didn't have a lot of respect for Jerry. The man had not left the building for more than fifteen years. He often paid the children who resided there to go shopping for him, and he had the other residents take care of his bills while they were out. Everyone said he had some kind of fear of the outside. Most people just helped him when they could. Walter hadn't lost respect for him because of that, but because he had gotten his job as the super of the building because he was related to the building's owner. At least, Jerry's sister was married to the man who owned the building. All in the family after all. Keep the jobs in the family, and keep the money there, too. Walter knew that one could

2

afford to have a paralyzing fear if one had options in life. Others had to do what they had to do. For Walter, that meant walking the pavement every single day looking for work, no matter what ailment he had that day.

"You know you're like two months behind, man. And I can't hold it off for much longer. Know what I'm saying, man?"

He honest to God hated when Jerry called him "man." He swore he heard "boy" every time. Every damn time. "I didn't get the job, Jerry. They were looking for somebody *less* qualified this time. Imagine that."

Jerry was quiet for a moment. "Sorry about that, man. So listen, I heard about this job. It's at the Ambassador. It's nothing high and mighty—a doorman or bellhop or whatever—but it's something..."

High and mighty? Walter didn't respond. If he did, he'd probably be jobless and homeless by the end of the day.

Jerry waited for a moment, as if letting the idea sink in, and then he continued. "The recession was over several months ago. Things are supposed to be better. What do you think the problem is?"

Maybe I just don't wanna work. Walter felt that the man was accusing him; he didn't like it, but he said simply: "What recession? This is pretty much what it's always looked liked from this side."

The rat had put a pretty good dent in the dried-up food covering the walls and floor by the time Walter got around to cleaning it up. The only things he had gained by throwing that pot were the giant cockroaches and a horde of ants. He had stopped at the corner store for some wire mesh to clog the hole that he had seen the rat come from, and now he spent two hours scouring the apartment for any other holes that even remotely looked like the rat could use to get back in. He plugged those up too. Then he set down to clean up the mess that he'd made. Several of the cockroaches were bold enough to climb up his pant leg, and he had to knock them off or drown them in the bucket of dirty water, the soap having long before turned to a mud-like consistency.

Of course, all this didn't do one bit of good. The rat came back the very same night, sniffing the floor for the food that Walter had already cleaned up. He had no idea how it was still getting in.

Walter ran over to the rat, stomping the floor, trying to crush the creature. He stomped around the apartment, the noise ringing through the thin walls of the building. The rat ran in circles, almost taunting him. Every time he'd lift his foot and bring it down, the rat would dodge him, running in another direction. The two danced back and forth like this for several minutes. Walter felt like a madman, stomping through the room this way, but he didn't care; he had to kill this thing. It was driving him crazy.

After what seemed like forever, Walter stopped, exhausted. He looked down just as the rat ran under the kitchen sink. He stood there, chest heaving up and down, defeated. He couldn't even kill a goddamn mouse. What good was he?

Walter was convinced that there were no jobs to be had in this godforsaken city. He wasn't a highly educated man, but he was smart enough to get by and he had lots of work experience. He had been at his previous job for almost ten years before the factory had closed down, shipping the jobs to other countries. He certainly hoped that at least those people could feed themselves and their families now, because he sure as hell couldn't. And forget a family. Walter had wanted one once. He had been in love, had wanted to get married. But none of that mattered anymore. He couldn't even feed himself, let alone a wife or children. His unemployment had run out the previous week, and he was down to the last of the stew. A few spoonfuls and he would be eating mayonnaise and mustard sandwiches, less the mayonnaise and mustard. And the bread.

Just two years before, Walter had had a decent house and job. He had been doing well. Then he lost his job, and the recession happened. Well, whatever they were calling it nowadays. The president had assured the country that a recession was when your neighbor lost his job. So since Walter's job had gone long ago, he supposed he was in an outright depression, as the president's words had implied. Either way, many of his white coworkers had found steady work, while Walter and the other blacks mostly seemed to struggle.

Recession, depression; who gave a shit? He just wanted to work. He still wanted an opportunity to find that shining city on a hill that was promised. He realized that perhaps this promise was not meant for him.

"I know I told you to come back this week and we may have

something for you," the guy from the unemployment office told him. "It's just hard right now. Most of the jobs are going to people who are skilled."

"I'm skilled," Walter had reminded him.

The man had looked at him like he'd grown a third leg. "I mean, unemployment has always been a problem in the black community. The jobs are just harder to find there."

"Then send me somewhere else. I can commute."

"If something comes up, you'll be the first to know. I promise." With that, Walter had been sent on his way. Three weeks later, nothing had come up.

Walter sat in the chair watching the rat wander his apartment, its small claws scratching the hardwood floor—or what passed for hardwood in this dump. He was sure that the thing had gotten fatter since he'd seen it last, only a day ago. Its fur looked thicker and shinier, too. As it sniffed the ground, every few seconds it would stop, standing on its hind legs, its front legs scratching the air, its nose and whiskers twitching wildly.

He had been right. This thing was getting fatter off his leavings. It was a fucking parasite. Walter flew out of his seat and pounced at the rat. He landed on the floor in the exact spot that the rat had been just a few moments before. He lay still for a moment, listening. Where had it gone? Just as he was getting ready to give up in frustration, he heard it. A quiet sound; a soft squeak from the tiny rodent. He tried to make himself as still as the apartment around him; he didn't even breath. The sound came again. Then the pain.

A sharp sensation in his flesh, claws burrowing into his chest. He had landed directly on the creature, and it had clawed its way through his untucked shirt, tearing the soft of his belly. Walter jumped to his feet, running around the room, his hands holding the bottom of his shirt closed. He had the bastard and he wasn't gonna let it go. He didn't care how bad it wounded him.

The rat crawled around beneath his shirt, wiggling and squirming. Walter jumped up and down in a strange dance that resembled something like a waltz and the mambo combined. He grabbed at the outside of his shirt, trying to get a hold of the rodent. The thing was quick and he kept missing it, grabbing only handfuls of fabric. Walter's skin felt like confetti and small trickles of blood began seeping through the cloth. After a while, he slipped his hands under his shirt and caught a piece of the rat's long tail. He pulled it out as the rat's claws tried desperately to hold onto his flesh. Finally, he ripped it away, taking chunks of his own flesh with it.

But he didn't care, he had it.

Walter held it by its tail in one hand and wrapped his other around the rat's thick body. As soon as he's gotten a good grip on it, he yelled in victory. He didn't know what he planned to do with the creature, but he finally had it. It bit him hard on his index finger. Walter screamed again, and the feeling of victory abated. He grabbed a wiggling front leg and pulled as hard as he could. The pressure popped the rat's leg right out of the socket and tore the limb from its body. Blood gushed from the open wound, and the rat made an awful squeaking noise.

As it wiggled and fought to get away, blood covering everything, it slithered out of Walter's hands and fell to the ground. It crawled slowly away, leaving a trail of blood behind. Walter stared at the small appendage in his left hand. He closed his hand and walked back to his seat. The rat would probably just bleed to death in the walls. He fondled the limb, then put it in his pocket. He had won.

The landlord pounded on the door about fifteen minutes later. Walter opened the door, not really looking at the man, his clothes and hair in shambles.

Jerry looked stunned. "What the hell is going on here, man? Your neighbors are complaining."

Walter knew that his neighbors from downstairs had moved out a month before, and the woman next door was deaf, so the only person complaining was Jerry. Walter didn't really give a damn. He hoped he had kept the man from doing something really important, like evicting some poor soul. Jerry took a moment to look him over.

"What happened to you, man?"

Walter didn't answer.

"Are you okay? My God, is that blood?"

Walter looked down at his clothing as if noticing for the first time. He nodded his head, "It's blood."

"Shit, man, you need me to call an ambulance?"

"No. That goddamn rat is taking over the building."

Jerry stared at him, not blinking, "We had the exterminator

here a few weeks ago. I told you then, ain't nobody seen no rats but you. But I called him anyway. You know they came out and sprayed everything."

"Well, I got 'im. It ain't gonna be bothering nobody no more."

Jerry looked into the apartment. Walter stepped into the hall and closed the door behind him.

Jerry sighed, "Found a job, man?"

"No job yesterday and no job today."

"Okay, Walter. Okay."

It was sitting on his dresser, nursing its wounded leg when Walter woke up the next morning. He sat up quickly and looked for something to finish the thing off with. His alarm clock was buzzing and the noise was an irritant in the otherwise silent room. The rat was blocking the clock, so Walter couldn't shut it off. The two simply stared at each other. Walter slowly slid from under the covers and walked around to unplug the clock. He picked up his shoe. He would beat the thing to death. That would do it.

Walter raised the shoe above the rat's head, then stopped, his hand dangling midair. It stared at him. He lowered his arm. "What in the hell...?"

"I dance, too." The rat spoke. Talked. Its little mouth moved as each word poured from its lips.

Walter backed away until he hit the bedroom wall. "Jesus!"

"Can you dance?" the rat asked.

Walter didn't answer. He was stunned. Shocked. *Hallucinating.* That was it. He was just imagining, or better yet, dreaming this, and he was still in his bed sleeping.

"Well, do you? Dance? Shuffle? Come on, man, speak up. Can you shuffle?"

Walter couldn't speak, so he just shook his head, no.

The rat hung his head. "That's too bad, really. A good shuffle is what you people need, ya know?"

Walter still couldn't bring himself to speak to the rat. Instead, he smacked himself, trying to wake up. He had put way too much attention into this rat of late, and now he'd even started dreaming of it. He had to snap out of it, get the hell out of this apartment, and do something. He didn't know what. Hell, he didn't actually have the money to even catch a movie, but he should go somewhere, do something. Get out of this damned apartment.

The problem was that Walter was knocking the hell outta himself, and he was still standing in the same spot, looking at the same talking rat. He hadn't woken up. He was stuck somewhere between an awful dream and reality. Sleepwalking. He'd heard of people doing all kinds of things while they were asleep. Maybe that was what was happening to him. But didn't those people always remain sleeping, not knowing they were awake?

"Wha... what do... you want?"

The rat looked at him and held up its missing limb.

Walter didn't understand. "You... you want it back?"

"Want it back? What the hell would I do with a severed leg? No, I don't want it back."

"Then what do you want?"

"Truce."

"So what's your name, Slick?"

Walter had climbed back into bed and pulled the covers up to his neck. He still couldn't bring himself to talk to this thing. The rat hopped from the nightstand to his bed and stood on his blanket, facing him. "They call me King. You know. Like the head honcho."

Walter just stared.

King began walking back and forth on all three legs, jumping over creases in the blanket. He was pacing, waiting for Walter to speak. But Walter was speechless, and even if the man could talk, he wasn't sure that he wanted to do it to this walking, talking king of rats. King crawled back toward Walter, stopping in front of him again.

"Man, you are a quiet one, indeed. I got an idea."

"Go away," Walter whispered. "Please go away." Sane people don't talk to rats. Sane people don't hear rats talk to them.

"Come on, let's play," King said.

"P... play?"

"Let's play white."

Walter couldn't get his ass out of that apartment fast enough. He dashed from under his thin, worn covers, grabbed his shirt, shoes and keys, and slammed the door behind him. Didn't put on decent pants—he still wore his pajama bottoms—or stop to put on his shoes until he was out in the street. He'd run down the five flights of stairs barefoot, his chest exposed like a damn fool. Luckily, his sleepwear was an old pair of sweats that he'd had for several years. He hadn't even bothered to comb his hair or brush his teeth, and he probably looked like a homeless man. But shit, he didn't care. He needed to get the hell away from that... thing taking over his house.

Now that he was out in the fresh air, not cramped up in his stale apartment, he tried to think. What in the hell had that rat been talking about? Had it been mocking Walter? What did it mean *let's play white*? What did King want from him?

On the corner, he stopped and stared at passersby. He didn't know where he was or how long he'd walked to get to this completely different neighborhood—nothing looked familiar anymore. He watched the faces and they watched him, cautious. Somehow, he had walked himself right out of his comfortable neighborhood of stoic black resolve and into foreign territory. The people here smiled, just not at him.

Walter looked down at his clothing and sighed. Just his luck he would be caught out of his house looking like this, in this neighborhood. At home, most people wouldn't even care, and they certainly wouldn't give him the nasty looks he was getting now. His vision blurred; he still hadn't cleared his head yet.

That damn rat had done this to him.

Walter stood with his back against the brownstone building, not feeling completely safe to walk on his own anymore. He knew he might be losing his mind, but he didn't want to admit it to himself. He probably needed to go see someone, explain everything to them. Explain what? That he'd been having a conversation with a rat named King? They would put him away for sure.

He stood there for a long time, trying to melt into the wall, become invisible. The people pushed by him, pretending they didn't see him while keeping an eye on him. He didn't care. He needed to rest a moment. He closed his eyes, raised his head up to the sky. Rested. Then someone ran into him. Just as he opened his eyes, a tall thin white woman fell to the ground at his feet, the contents of her purse spilling to the ground. Change, light-colored makeup, and lipstick scattered across the cement. Walter bent down to help her.

He didn't think about it; it was a natural reaction. He should have known better. As the woman saw him bending over her, she screamed. Suddenly the whole sidewalk was alive with people staring at the pair.

He was frozen, hands reached out toward what even to him looked like the woman's throat. The sea of white faces stared at him. "I... I was just gonna..."

"No—no—no—" The woman screamed, her voice ringing out over the clustered buildings. "Safe space. Safe space."

Walter stared, speechless. She yelled again, louder, repeating her words. He stood up, walked forward, his hands open, surrendering. "Lady. Calm down. I..."

Several people walked over to the woman, and she crawled between their legs, trying to get away from him. Someone touched his shoulder. As he turned, Walter looked directly into the eyes of a policeman.

"Can you come with me please, sir?"

"What'd I...?" Walter still couldn't piece together a coherent sentence.

The officer looked down at the open purse and then back at him. "Don't make a scene in front of these good folks. Please just come with me."

It hadn't been easy trying to convince the police that Walter hadn't tried to rob and rape the white woman. They'd asked him what he was doing in that neighborhood and how he had gotten there and why he'd come. Of course he couldn't answer any of the questions honestly, so he'd said he'd just been out for a jog. They hadn't believed him. Then they tried to reason with him. They completely understood his situation and it had all been an accident, so if he just admitted it, then they would let him go. Walter almost fell for it. But there was nothing to admit. That was okay, the officers had said, just sign *this paper* and he would be let go. Walter wasn't the best educated man, but he could read. The paper was a confession.

His saving grace, ironically enough, had come from the crazy rambling "Safe space" woman. After calming down, she had admitted that she had been pushed into Walter and that she had panicked because she had been robbed only a few days before—by a black man. So, it was only natural that she was scared of Walter, she explained.

King was waiting for Walter when he walked in the door fourteen hours later. For the life of him, Walter was happy to see him—to see and talk to anyone. The rat sat on his nightstand, rubbing his wounded stump while Walter explained his ordeal. When Walter was finished, King didn't say anything for a long time. The two sat there, each seemingly in his own thoughts.

"So, you wanna play?"

Walter didn't respond. He was tired.

After a while, the rat king spoke: "You gotta get with the program, Slick. You gotta understand what you're dealing with, see. Acquiesce, man." He paused for a moment, letting the realization sink into Walter. Still, the man did not say anything. Walter looked around and for a moment, the room seemed to be getting smaller. He couldn't breathe; the air was thick and dirty. He wondered if this rodent had some kind of airborne disease. Perhaps in a few hours Walter would be dying right there in that room and King would not even wait for him to take his last breath before he started to gnaw on Walter's still-living flesh. Perhaps it would be payback for his severed limb. Then the rat would look at him, and while Water died, King would proclaim victory. "I have won," King would say.

But now that Walter thought about it, he didn't care. Sure, it would hurt to be eaten alive, but at least, in the end, he would be dead. It would be over and he wouldn't have to worry about anything anymore. No job; who'd care? No money; not important. No food; can't starve to death if you're already dead. No police, no more fighting for that piece of invisible pie; now that was a plus.

Walter had always thought that the pie was big enough to go around for everyone. Everyone had the same chance to claw his way to the American Dream, right? After all, he had been born a poor black boy in the south, but he had made it to factory foreman within ten years. All because he worked hard and fought, right? But it hadn't taken much for all that to crumble. In fact, in Walter's view, the very idea of fighting to the top meant that you had to fight others to get there. Or worse, that you had to leave people behind on your way.

King stared at him, his rat eyes wide. He seemed to be waiting for Walter to come to some kind of realization. Acquiesce, as the rat had put it. *Acquiesce.*

"So, you wanna play, then?" The rat paused, gave him time to think. "I'll start. Well, sir, I do declare, it is a very fine evening we are having, wouldn't you say? The weather is quite marvelous."

Walter stared at King and said nothing. He didn't move, didn't blink. *Acquiesce*, huh? He couldn't see the harm in it. What the hell. He didn't care anymore. Walter put on his most well-refined white voice, the one he used for interviews, and responded. "Indeed it is, sir. A lovely evening."

"And how's life treating you, sir?"

"Can't complain."

As it stood, the following day was indeed a fine one. The weather was quite marvelous and the sun was shining. Of course it had been shining for three weeks straight, as there had been no rain, but Walter hadn't noticed. But there were no complaints from him now.

He stopped at Jerry's door on the way back to his apartment. The man took a long time to answer. Walter knew he was there, because he hardly ever left his apartment and it was even rarer (as in it had never happened in the two years that Walter had lived there) for him to venture out past the front doors of the building. So Walter knocked again. Waited.

Finally, Jerry opened the door. He looked tired, drained. "How's it going, man?"

"Good. You?"

"Okay, man."

"Good."

Jerry looked down the hall, both ways, then back at Walter. He always did that, as if he thought someone was waiting to jump him. "So what can I do you for, man?"

"Just wanted to let you know that I got a job. I start Monday, and I should be able to pay ya something a week or so after that."

Jerry smiled. "That is good news. I was getting worried. Thought I was gonna have to put you out in the street. Man..."

"Okay, then." Walter left him standing in the doorway.

King was sitting on the counter when he walked in the door.

Walter walked past him and plopped into his chair facing the kitchen. He didn't say anything to King, and the rat, in turn, seemed to want to give him a moment to collect himself. Walter took off his shoes and threw them into the corner. They landed in the spot that was most likely King's entrance and exit point, but Walter was never quite sure how the rat got into the apartment. He had given up trying to find out. What did it even matter, anymore? He lay his head back, staring at the ceiling, and sighed.

"Well?" said King. Clearly, the rat had had all he could take. He needed to hear the words.

"I got the job."

"Great, man. What job? What will you be doing?"

"Doorman."

"See?" the rat said. "You won after all."

Walter fingered the severed rat's foot that he kept in his pocket, kissed it, and placed it back for safe keeping. *You won*, King's scratchy voice repeated in his head. The man sighed. *Would that it were true.*

"PURSE"

Manyara Ashu clenched her purse tightly, as if it possessed gold or silver, her soft, sullen features twinkling in the dull subway lights. Behind her, a gust of wind picked up, signaling an oncoming train and blowing her dark hair into wild tangles. She seemed not to notice; she stood and waited quietly for her ride.

On the train she shuffled to her seat—evidence of a long workday with no end in sight. In fact, many of the transit's daily participants had the same limp, which seemed to worsen as the days wore into weeks and years. The bitter aroma of urine floated up her nose, but she paid it no mind—she had smelled it before on these trains.

She stared at other passengers on the car, certain that any one of them might be ready to grab her valuable bag at any moment. This would be no surprise; riding the subway in New York was always a risk, which many were willing to take on a day-to-day basis as long as it got them to and from where they were going on time. Sweat broke out on her face and rolled down her temple to her shoulder and snaked slowly down her body.

At the far end of the car, a group of four teen thugs laughed and played, a stream of violent profanities spilling from their youthful lips. Most of them sported colors of a local gang and made appropriate finger gestures. They all looked menacing enough, but none of them had even bothered to look at her or her special belongings. For this she was grateful.

Across from her, a man and a woman held each other. As he whispered sweet nothings into her ear, she giggled and covered her mouth, hoping no one would hear. The woman was dressed nicely—in clothes Manyara could never afford—and she carried herself discreetly and with elegance. She wore valuable rings and held her hand in phony half-waves to show them off. A Manhattan woman, Manyara thought. But her dark skin was a definite sign of the woman's stature, and she would never be able to escape that.

The man, too, was a fake with his fifty-dollar suit and two hundred-dollar shoes. Manyara was sure that she saw a wedding ring on his finger, but none on the woman's. Perhaps the Manhattan woman was not as valuable as she thought.

In the seat directly facing hers was a tall black man. His clothes were faded and dirty and sweat stained the armpits of his work shirt. His boots were caked with clay dirt and double-tied at the ankles. She guessed he was some kind of construction worker. His face was stern and he hadn't smiled since he boarded the train—but hell, neither had she. No one did on a New York subway; you just knew better. He stared at her almost hatefully, and she pretended not to notice.

Please don't take my purse, she thought, the man's eyes still concentrating on her as she saw his reflection in the window.

The train car hit a bump just as it entered a tunnel; the lights flickered and went out completely. She sat there in the dark—for what to her seemed like forever—and saw the man's shadow rise from its seat and loom over her. He was a giant of sorts; at least it looked that way in the dark. She swallowed hard, trying not to scream.

She repeated in her mind, *Please don't take my purse*, the man's shadow only feet from her.

Manyara had gotten paid only a few days before, and she carried a large amount of money with her. She didn't feel safe leaving it at home, not in her neighborhood. And since her husband had abandoned her a few months before (he needed his space, he couldn't take care of a family, he had said), she didn't feel safe there herself. She also carried her apartment key, her wallet with her identification, and a few other priceless goodies.

The lights snapped back on. As her eyes grew accustomed to the brightness, she noticed that the man had indeed moved to a seat closer to her; now he sat in the one just opposite of hers.

Please don't take it. It never occurred to Manyara that perhaps the man was after something more precious to her than that damned purse. She never thought that maybe, just maybe, he wanted to steal the priceless valuables that she kept safely hidden under her skirt and between her ebony legs. The one thing her husband had always called his "special place." It never occurred to her that this big construction builder might have wanted something more important. But at that moment there was nothing more important to her in the whole world than that bag. Her life was in there: her money, wallet, and her cherished private things.

The purse weighed heavy on her shoulder, and she held it with all the strength she had in her. Her pretty hazel eyes twinkled in fear, and she wiped away the crust forming in the corner of one of them.

The man stared at her lustfully.

Her hands and uncovered legs began to drip with sweat. The train operator's voice boomed through the speaker as he announced the next stop.

Oh good, mine is next. As the bell rang for final call, just before the doors closed, Manyara readied herself for departure. She dropped her heavy load to the floor.

The man leaned in and touched her.

She jumped back and crumpled into the seat. "Please don't." Her voice sounded soft, faint, as foreign to her as the man's hand on her thigh.

He spoke: "Ma'am, are you all right?"

She didn't answer; didn't hear.

"Ma'am?"

"Don't take it," she whispered.

"Are you okay? You're bleeding."

Manyara lay there repeating over and over again in her head, *Please don't take my purse.* She so desperately wanted to hang onto her precious secret.

Droplets of dark red blood flowed from a hidden wound under her dress. "You're bleeding. Is there anything I can do?" the man asked again. She continued to lie there, the pain in her heart evident on her face.

By now, the few other passengers that were still on the train had joined the black man. The blood flow had increased and a tiny puddle lay between her legs.

"Ma'am? Can you hear me?"

Nothing.

"What can I do? Are you hurt?"

From behind the man, the Manhattan woman picked up Manyara's purse and opened it. She screamed.

"Just don't take it," Manyara pleaded.

Inside the purse, a tiny, bloody baby lay curled tightly, almost hugging itself, among discarded papers and bits and pieces of Manyara's unimportant personal effects, staring at the world through dead eyes.

But none so eerie as Manyara's as she lay there, tears tumbling down her soft, dark face.

"It's all I've got in the world."

"I Make People Do Bad Things"

Old Sam was dying. He had been dying for approximately twenty-seven years, by Queenie's account. Exactly the amount of time since hell had frozen over and God had relinquished the title on His throne, if the old man thought she was gonna let him slide by on another number without paying her proper due.

"Come on, Madam St. Clair, help out an old, dying man. I ain't got long now, you know."

"You old fool, if you think you're getting anything else from me on credit, you're all balled up."

The old man looked at her, seemed to want to respond, then thought better of it and hung his head. *Shit,* the old bastard owed her more than a dollar for bets that he hadn't been able to cover. Now he thought she would let him slide by again. No way in hell.

The door to her operation on 144th Street, between Lenox and Seventh Avenue, swung open. Bumpy Johnson, her head enforcer, pushed past Sam and dumped a large package on the floor. It wiggled. Bumpy kicked it, nodded to her. She walked over, unwrapped it. A bloody white man lay on the floor staring up at her.

"Mr. Johns. Comme c'est gentil á vous de faire notre connaissance." Queenie would never admit it out loud, but she loved to use her knowledge of French to intimidate people. It made her feel smarter than these silly Americans, superior. In this case she had said nothing more than *How nice of you to make our acquaintance,* but the man cowered at her feet as if she had threatened to slice his throat and leave him sleeping with the fishes. That was certainly not outside of the realms of possibility.

Sam stared for only a moment, then rushed to the door and opened it.

"Old Sam?" The man stopped, looked at her. "That number was 216, right?"

He nodded.

"I'll play you."

The old man smiled, looked down at the man on the floor and his smile faded. Then he quickly shuffled out the door.

Queenie turned slowly to the man at her feet. "Unfortunately for you, Mr. Johns, vous ne vous en tirez pas si *facilement.*"

The numbers racket was Madam St. Clair's business. She ran everything in all of Harlem, from Washington Heights to the Upper East Side, from the East River to the Hudson River—it all belonged to her. Ten thousand dollars from her own pocket had begun this business, and now it was her pocket into which all proceeds went. Less overhead, of course. Part of that overhead, and worth every thin dime that she paid them, was Bumpy and her gang of Forty Thieves. They were ruthless, and with her guidance they ran the streets with strict precision that was almost surgical.

The numbers business was simple. One came into any of her many establishments—grocery markets, pool halls, restaurants, drugstores; if you owned a business in Harlem and you were willing to make a little extra dough, you took numbers—bet on any number between 0 and 999, and waited. Called the "poor man's stock market," it was bound to pay off. Where there were numbers running in Harlem, those uptown guys played the real thing and often lost big. Here, the odds paid out eight to one. Pretty good, and Madam St. Clair always paid. There was no business in undercutting your clientele. If you played long and often enough, you eventually won. So people played and she got rich.

For most people in Harlem, the numbers game was a way of making a few extra dollars during the month. For others it meant surviving: eating or not eating. People put down a dime, a nickel, or even a penny and hoped for a payout. A dollar could have a return of six hundred dollars—no wonder this was big business. No wonder she'd made a fortune.

But the people in the neighborhood adored her; playing the odds had fed many people when it wouldn't have otherwise been possible. She also provided hundreds of jobs when there were none to be had in the outside world. So she had affectionately become known as Queenie—as in the Queen of Harlem—and she relished it. She fought every day to keep the title and her reign. It wasn't easy. She had to be ruthless, heartless, and deathly to survive.

Madam St. Clair was all of those things. Most importantly, she was a *she.*

And *they* didn't like that.

Behind her, Bumpy walked in, closed the door behind him, and placed his hand on her shoulder. He never showed her affection unless they were alone. He didn't speak for a long time, and she was content to let the silence stand. But she knew that he would say what was on his mind; she even knew, for the most part, what it was. He squeezed her shoulder blade, massaging her, his fingers feeling good against her flesh, comfortable.

Finally, he spoke, his voice soft. "Johns belongs to the Irish. We going to war with them too, now? I really hope you know what you're doing, Madam. I miss h..."

She swung to look at him. He would never have spoken to her like this if others were around; he would have known better. One didn't show dissention in the ranks publicly. But in private, things were different. He was close to her, too close. He knew her. However, she could not let this slide. He knew that, too. "You a chicken-shit, Bumpy?"

It was harsh, but equal to the disrespect he had shown her. He stayed calm. "You know I'm not. I do what you tell me, always have. I just want to make sure we know what we're doing, is all."

"Of course I know what we're doing. We're starting war."

Bumpy squeezed her arm once more and walked out of the room, closing the door quietly behind him. Once he was outside, he would have to quiet the others who were afraid of Shultz's retaliation. He would do it, for if even one person brought their concerns to her, she would not wait until Shultz got his hands on them. There was a price to be in her favor, and cowards were not tolerated. Not that there were many of those in her gang of forty.

Queenie hung her head. How had things gotten to this point? How had she allowed them to get so out of control? *To hell with them for what they've done.* It was too late now. It couldn't be changed.

Shiv. The word hovered in Queenie's mind, unspoken. But the woman couldn't forget.

In the beginning, street traffic got heavy to her club around seven in the evening, after work. People needed to play after long hours at tedious jobs, and she provided entertainment. Gambling. Dancing. Booze. Girls. The cutest little quiffs you could find, and for decent prices. That was what she did, what she was good at.

You name it; people wanted it. You name it; she offered it.

Not quite as big and elaborate as her establishment now, Madam's had Place catered to a low grade clientele. But there had been hardly any trouble. People had respected her just as they did now, although she hadn't wielded nearly as much power then. The only difference was that her power back then came from what lay between the legs of her girls. Period. She hadn't liked it, but she'd accepted it. Queenie had promised herself that as soon as she had the opportunity she would get the hell out of that business and find something more respectable. She had made that promise on her knees every single day.

Ellsworth "Bumpy" Johnson had come to her highly recommended. He wore pinstriped, three-piece suits with $200 shoes. His ties always matched his mood. Red meant angry, ready to fight. Blue, one could possibly have a chance, as he was happy. Black was death. In the beginning he had done odd jobs for her, bounced people out on their asses when they ran out of money, collected on high interest and overdue loans, protected the girls. That was what he did, and he was damn good at it.

Shiv was the daughter of one of her girls. Shiv's mother, Lutie, had gotten herself sick, so the girl took over as much as she could to make up for her mother's shortcomings. The girl swept up, got the quiffs what they needed, but mainly stayed out of the way. It was important for Shiv to scram when the marks were around because, although Queenie knew most of her clientele, unsavory people often wandered in, and a young girl had no business being around that sort. Even so, she was a quiet girl. She didn't talk to the marks. She didn't talk to the girls. She talked to her mother. She was an enigma to Queenie for several reasons, and that never really changed. Queenie had come to regret that.

Shiv. The child hadn't always been called that, but Queenie had long since forgotten the girl's original name. Shiv, once given, had been so true and exact that nothing else had mattered. It had cemented her place among the group. The old woman laughed to herself; a girl of nine years had become a member of the Forty Thieves, one of the deadliest gangs in Harlem. Queenie herself couldn't quite believe it.

Queenie had always been under threat of violence before her gang grew to the size it was now. She paid the cops, she paid the greasers; she paid, it seemed, everyone. Even that wasn't enough, as several people still came in, getting their fill of girls and her money as they wished. The worst of these was Doc Marsh, a halfwit thug who thought he ran the East Side. Queenie reasoned the man wasn't really all that smart, but he had a baby grand of muscle behind him, and together the group was just dangerous enough to be trouble for her.

It was Doc Marsh who came to her joint that night. He was drunk when he arrived, and he got more and more zozzled as the night went on. Queenie had just advised the girls, as usual, to be nice and deal with him. For the most part, this strategy worked. Not that night.

It hadn't taken long for Doc Marsh to spot Lutie. The woman was a choice bit of calico, an absolute doll. Dark chocolate skin and large beautiful eyes that shone like Scotch whiskey; that was Lutie. But she was off limits. Sick and getting sicker by the day. Lutie had been working around the club, cleaning up after the girls, doing the dirty work that nobody wanted in an effort to keep Queenie from doing what they both knew was inevitable.

Doc Marsh grabbed the woman, pulled her onto his lap. He kissed her. Several of the girls alerted Queenie to what was happening. Before Queenie could intervene, Lutie pushed away from Doc and said calmly, "Sorry, Mac. Bank's closed." This should have stopped him—most customers understood; most wouldn't've wanted any more hassle. Not Doc Marsh. When Lutie tried to pull away again, the man wrestled with her, threw her on the table and bit her on the cheek, leaving a smear of blood trickling down her face. Lutie was a pro; she didn't scream, but she kneed him in the groin and he staggered backward. When he regained his footing, he charged the woman again, punched her across the face, and kicked her when she bent over in pain. Suddenly Bumpy got between Lutie and Doc Marsh.

By the time Doc's men arrived to help him, most of the trouble was over. Doc was, as usual, still lathered. He screamed about an invisible wound that he swore Lutie had inflicted. He screamed and made himself the fool. "That bitch. I swear, I will—" Lutie stood upright, stared at Doc as he spoke, didn't back down. But she didn't challenge him, either. She knew better. This seemed to egg the man on. "I swear, I want her gone. Do you hear—" he pointed to Queenie "—gone."

Finally, when he grew tired, he decided to leave. Just as he turned, Shiv blocked his way, her tiny dark body swallowed by the large white man. He almost bumped into her, stopping himself in a drunken swivel. Just as he moved again to leave, the girl reached out and deliberately ran a finger across the chest of his double-breasted suit. Doc Marsh looked down at the girl, eyes wide as if he questioned his sight. Finally, he turned to look at Queenie, pointed again at Lutie, and then stormed out, his flunkies right at his heels.

Who did that bastard think he was? He didn't own her, or her club. She paid him and he believed he got the run of the place? But as she thought about it, the man was right. At this point it would be best for all of them if the woman and her daughter left. She had been dreading this moment, but she had known it would come. It was business. Lutie and that child were a liability. And Doc wouldn't let it go.

The following day she told Lutie. "I gotta do it. I know you ain't got nowhere to go and I know you're sick. But, you can't work and Doc Marsh ain't gonna forget. And you got a daughter. He ain't civilized. Ain't no telling what he'll do."

The woman nodded, but she was crying. Then her daughter came in and held her mother. Queenie stared at the pair. Lutie looked terrible. Her eyes were sunken, bruised. Not because of the shiner that Doc had given her—it was her sickness; it was consuming her. She wouldn't last long. Queenie knew it. Lutie knew. Most of all, Shiv knew.

"I can pay our due," the girl said. She didn't stand more than four and a half feet off the ground, but in that moment, Queenie swore she looked like a grown woman. A nine-year-old girl had no business worrying about her dying mother. A nine-year-old had no business in this place.

"No."

"Please," the girl begged, and she began to resemble the child that she was. "We ain't got nowhere to go." She began to cry. "I can help. I know I can."

"Girl, ain't no way I'm putting a kid your age to work in no ho house. Take your momma and go, chile."

Shiv stomped over to her desk; she put her tiny dark hands on the stark white papers covering the old mahogany. "I make people do bad things."

"The hell you talking about, girl?"

Shiv straightened up, looked Queenie in the eyes, and for the first time, the girl resembled her future namesake. "Doc Marsh can't bother us no more. I fixed it. I...wish he'd jump. The bridge..." Before the girl could finish, Bobbie, one of Queenie's errand boys, busted in the door without knocking, his dark eyes bright with fear, or something that resembled fear.

Just as she was about to admonish him, the boy spoke. "Did ya hear? Doc Marsh, he's dead."

Queenie stood. "What?"

"Jumped off the High Bridge, landed, splat—" he smacked his hands together "—right on the highway."

Queenie looked from the boy to the girl, to Lutie and back at the girl. Shiv nodded, smiled.

"I did," she said.

She did. At least Shiv thought she did. And that was enough for Queenie. What were the odds of the girl having talked about Doc Marsh jumping off a bridge and then it happening? Queenie hadn't started dealing in numbers yet, but she was sure that those odds were pretty damned high. She wasn't one to believe in coincidence. At the same time, it didn't escape her that the girl could have heard it somehow, somewhere. Although, by all accounts it had only just happened, and Bobbie swore he had just learned about the man's death in the street.

Doc Marsh's death took a big strain off Queenie. Afterward, there had been no one to control the dead man's business, and his crew simply drifted apart. Oh, they'd tried to take over, but it was soon clear that the Doc had been the brains of that operation. Bumpy got rid of the rest of them quickly.

Queenie, for her part, wasn't one to look a gift horse in the mouth. Shiv had made it possible for her and her mother to stay, but now she had to earn her keep, as Bumpy kept reminding her. "We need her. If the girl can do what you say she can, then what can it hurt?"

What can it hurt? Indeed.

About this time, Casper Holstein, an unknown ex-vet, had done his stint downtown on Wall Street as a bellhop. He'd come away with the idea of running numbers and had amassed a fortune. Others were slowly beginning to make money as well. Numbers wasn't big business yet, but it had potential, as Bumpy kept reminding her. Queenie wasn't so sure. As much as she hated the business, she was comfortable dealing in girls. They were easy. Queenie had scouters out on the streets, approaching single girls getting off the bus alone, bringing them into the fold. It wasn't difficult to find starving, willing young women. They were waiting. She could probably live her whole life in that two-bit club bedding empty soldiers to broken girls. She thought of Lutie; but at what cost? What gain?

Numbers running was a man's game. Either it would pay off for her or she would lose everything. But something had to give.

Finally, when she was ready, she talked to Bumpy.

"Okay. What is this numbers business?" she asked him. He lay on her sofa, shirt unbuttoned to expose his chest. He had fallen asleep. "You play, right?"

He blinked his eyes. "It's good money. Pays well."

"Good investment?"

"Yeah."

"What we need?"

"Capital."

"I got ten thou," she said, as if praying to the Lord. "Good enough?"

He sat up, looked at her. "It's a hard business. Not like the girls—not that simple. We'll need a small army to run it. I have the men. Thirty-nine of them, just waiting for the go-ahead. The problem is that Small Sammie runs things on this side now. He's placed stakes. He won't take lightly to competition. We'd have to take care of him first."

She paused for a moment. At that point she had never willingly ordered the murder of another human being. This would be opening a new door, one she hoped she could close at will. "Let's do it."

Bumpy shook his head. "It's not that easy. Small is not easy to get to. I've...tried."

"What? You've tried?" Bumpy had never acted without her directive in the past.

He met her eyes when he spoke. "I knew that it was just a matter of time that you'd come to this decision. No disrespect, Madam."

She believed him. "Even so, don't do it again. I mean that, B."

He nodded, paused long enough to show proper respect, and then continued, "Small keeps well-guarded. Doesn't leave the house. I figure you don't want a massive shootout in the streets. But—" he paused, looked into her eyes "—we can use the girl."

She knew exactly which girl he was talking about, and she didn't like it. He must have read the reaction on her face, because he quickly added, "Just listen. We send her in as a house girl, she cleans, does the floors, whatever. She can do that. Then she does her thing, gets out quick. If he buys the farm, good. If not, no harm, no foul."

"I... I can't do that. It don't make no sense. She'll get killed."

"Not if she can do what you say she can. What *she* said she can."

"She's a child. They lie."

He nodded, looked at the floor, then back at her. "Madam, I have never told you how to run your business. And I don't mean to now. If you want me to declare outright war on this man before we have a stable business up and running, then I will. If you want me to stay here, work for you, I'll do that too. You tell me what you want."

So that was that. Queenie had given Shiv Small Sammie's name and a picture and sent her out for what Queenie had hoped would be a repeat of history. *A name and a picture.* That was it, all she had given the girl. Later, she discovered that Bumpy had given her a knife, just in case. For all the good it would do.

She was nine years old. NINE YEARS OLD. What kinda evil bitch sends a small child off to kill a man?

Madam "Queenie" St. Clair, that's who.

The three weeks the girl was gone were the longest of Queenie's life. She spent the time in the bed of one of her favorite whores. This woman could make a man forget his miseries; she did the same for Queenie, among other things. Somehow it comforted Queenie to have her soft body close, made her feel like less of a monster. She avoided Bumpy and blamed him for the choices they both had made. It was easier that way.

The day Shiv came back, Small Sammie was run over by a train in upstate New York. No one knew how he had gotten there or what had happened. The moment the girl walked through the front door, Bumpy picked her up and swung her around. He hadn't said anything about the girl while she was gone, but Queenie guessed that he'd been worried about her. She hadn't noticed, but perhaps the man had avoided her as much as she had avoided him, both lost in guilt.

Shiv, for her part, beamed accomplishment. Word hadn't gotten around about Small's death yet, but nobody cared whether the girl had actually done what she said or not. She was back, alive. That was all that mattered. Once word did come in that Small Sammie was dead, no one could believe it. Three days later, news got around that he'd been hit by a train, pretty much at the exact moment that Shiv had walked back through Queenie's doors—and just as the girl told them he would.

Bumpy seemed most proud, as if he'd birthed a baby killer. "She's as deadly as a weapon. I don't know what you do, girl, but you're more deadly than a shiv, more accurate and less messy. My baby shiv."

And it stuck. Shiv: the child that turned killer. From that moment on, Shiv was Bumpy's shadow; where there was Bumpy, there was Shiv, and vice versa.

Two things had happened while Shiv was gone: she had done her job and killed Small Sammie, and Lutie had died from "complications." Shiv, for her part, seemed to take the news remarkably well. She didn't cry. She wasn't angry. She had simply insisted on a funeral, and Momma St. Clair, as the girl began to call her, dished out five hundred bucks on her funeral. They buried the woman in a grave on the outskirts of town.

It rained during the funeral, and the girl bent down, her tiny hands touching the coffin, caressing the silver-colored box. Shiv spoke to her dead mother, but Queenie and the others couldn't hear what she said. When she was finished, Shiv turned to Queenie and opened her mouth to speak, but didn't. After a moment, the girl spoke to everyone standing there watching her, pimp and whores alike. She said, simply, "I see you."

For the first time, Queenie viewed the girl as a double-edged sword. Sure, she could kill for her, but the girl could also kill her and anyone else she desired, at any moment she desired it. What use was a weapon that volatile? *What happens when the child outgrows its parent?*

Queenie invested her money, started her business and it thrived. When the numbers business got off the ground, she put dress suits on the girls and sent them out on the corners to hustle numbers for her. They made more money running numbers than they ever had on their backs, and it was decent, respectable work. Her Forty Thieves and two dozen ex-whores worked magic on the corners of Harlem.

By this time, Dutch Schultz, a white mobster who distributed liquor during the Prohibition, had gotten a whiff of the money that could be made running numbers in black Harlem. He wanted a piece of the action, and he would kill to get it. Dutch had the cops and politicians in his pocket, and he began to wage war against her. Queenie had wanted to avoid blood in the streets, and she had, for a while. Eventually, though, it had been inevitable, and she supposed she had been naive in thinking that it was even possible to do so. Bumpy and her Forty Thieves had set the streets ablaze protecting her interest, killing Shultz's men in the process. In return, Shultz killed hers. Her only advantage was Shiv.

The girl was able to infiltrate Schultz's community where whole groups of his men would die off slowly, methodically. They would choke themselves to death on their own forks, step out in front of Mack trucks, shoot each other to death for no apparent cause; it didn't matter, they were dead and couldn't challenge Queenie. Shiv began to kill wiseguys with a frank regard that even scared Queenie. The girl withdrew. It was in her eyes. Always the indicator of a child's suffering, Shiv's were empty, devoid of anything, any emotion. Any empathy. Queenie enjoyed the money, the power. The people around her enjoyed the perks of that power. Her errand boys, her cooks, her cleaners, everyone won because of her success. Shiv gained more than most.

None of it seemed to make the child happy. And everyone, at this point, worked to make Shiv happy. They were afraid. When the girl wasn't around, people would whisper about her. When she was around, they benefited. Either way, Shiv didn't care, she wasn't happy. Queenie reasoned that happiness was all but impossible with her mother gone. Shiv had willingly worked for her when she thought she was protecting her mother. Now, that just couldn't happen.

Queenie had said that the girl was always an enigma to her, and this was true. But the woman believed that she knew Shiv because she knew herself; Queenie related to her as she related to the women like her. The women in this hopeless, useless place, this life. Shiv was every child, every woman who was never given another option.

Queenie hated herself a little more each day for what she'd done. Still, Shiv killed for her.

Queenie hadn't been there the day it happened. Story went that one of the Thieves, Bumpy's right hand man, Hurts, had made the mistake. Hurts was a big man. He dressed like he bought all his clothes out of a secondhand shop, but he was brutal. He carried a baseball bat and would beat the hell out of men who annoyed him in the streets. A short fuse did not mix well with her new establishment. Not with Shiv.

The man had disrespected the girl's position in the Thieves. Shiv didn't care about a lot of things, but she had earned her way into the gang, and she would not accept anything less. Bumpy had named her, and she deserved it. If Queenie had been there, she would have had Hurts' tongue torn out, but that wasn't his luck. Shiv walked up to the big man, who sat laughing at the girl, and slid her fingers across his face, as a baby would. The next day, Hurts sliced off his dick with a rusted shiv. He bled to death in the alley behind Queenie's new place.

The following week, two more of the Forty Thieves died after having run-ins with Shiv. Everything Queenie had built was falling apart. On the business side, Schultz had gotten to the police, and despite having paid them off, the cops began harassing her, and placed nearly half of her men in jail. Including Bumpy.

The following week, Madam St. Clair walked into the newspaper office and placed an ad in the paper detailing the corruption of the police force, all of the monies that she had paid them, and whom she had paid. Her business might fall apart, but she would take as many people with her as she could.

The day Bumpy was let out of jail, Queenie received a letter from Schultz himself. She met him in an alley, off the record, as he had said.

"I know about the girl." Dutch Schultz always looked like he was waiting to take a mug shot. His eyes were large and sat too far apart on his head. He was a Jew—Jews and blacks didn't mix.

"The hell you say?"

"The nigger girl who you keep as some kinda lucky charm or something."

Queenie just stared at him.

"You know what I'm talking about, bitch."

Queenie made a circular motion with her hands, and she, Bumpy, and what was left of her men moved to walk away.

"Wait." Shultz called after her. He ran to her, his men staring, surprised. "I'm sorry. Please hear me out. I... I want a truce."

She stopped, looked at him.

"You keep Harlem. I get a cut." She started to protest, but he continued. "You can expand further out, have more territory. More money than you've ever dreamed. I'll get the cops off your back, the people uptown too."

"What do you want?"

"The girl."

"No."

"I know you have lost men. Several. You could lose more. You could...die too. Does she mean that much to you? Think about it."

The woman looked at Bumpy, who turned his head. She couldn't tell if it was in disgust or reluctant acceptance. "I want the body."

The white men shot Shiv down in the streets two weeks later. Queenie buried her in a plot next to her mother. It didn't rain. No one but Queenie and Bumpy mourned for the child. The women who had helped to raise the girl were too fearful by this point, and they had all simply wanted it over. Queenie had given it to them. She believed that they all felt guilty. She did.

A year later, Dutch Schultz was gunned down at the Palace Chop House restaurant in Newark, New Jersey. He was in the hospital, dying of his wounds.

Queenie sat down, placed her head in her hands. After a long while, she opened her drawer, took out pen and paper. She wrote simply, *Qui sème le vent, récolte la tempéte.* "As ye sow, so shall ye reap." She addressed the envelope to the hospital in care of Dutch Schultz and called for Bumpy.

"Send this by telegram." She handed the letter to the man, who stared at it suspiciously. Finally, she said, "After you mail that, let Johns go with a message: I'm out." Bumpy smiled briefly, but long enough for her to recognize his out-of-form expression. Then he nodded and walked out of the room.

LET'S PLAY WHITE

Queenie stared at her place; thought of the much smaller one from which she had come. Thought about the little girl, Shiv.

I make people do bad things, the girl had once said.

Moi aussi, Queenie thought. *So do I.*

"The Unremembered"

In the beginning, there was the Sun and Africa and there were those put here to remember and record. Oral scribes—griots—whose jobs were to act as a collective memory for an entire nation. But to forget is to cause injury to one's self and one's people. To forget is to be lost in thoughts of nothing. To forget knowledge is a sin.

The girl writhed in pain, lost to all around her. Her thoughts and actions had long been taken over by something she could not control. Her body, a lump of dead mass, her arms and legs moving to the beat of their own drum—that drum, pain. The aches took over not long before, and it didn't matter any longer that she could not move, could not talk. She learned a long time ago that being lost in her own mind was simply the way things were, at least for her. Those outside noises and voices—many of them she thought she could remember if she just tried hard enough—were still simply on the periphery, speaking to a body that did not respond. One that could not respond, even if it wanted to—and it certainly did not want to.

Her name was Jeli. She knew this not because of those voices outside her head, but because of the ones inside, the ones speaking to her. She knew this because it was told to her. She was told she'd been put here to suffer—and suffer, she did.

Jeli's black body twisted and contorted in a way that would not have been possible if she'd had full control over her limbs. Her mother knew this, but all she could do was hold the girl in her arms. Nosipha, the girl's mother, said a silent prayer to whomever might be listening at the time. A sin, of course—one should pray to God and God alone—but it seemed as if the Lord himself had stopped answering her prayers a long time ago, so she supposed it would not hurt to ask all those with knowledge of her daughter's pain to aid her.

Something in her daughter's head broke and the girl stretched out, stiff as a board, and screamed with such fury the woman jumped despite herself. As she gathered her senses, she noticed what caused the girl's anguish. A thin, circular ring of blood appeared around her daughter's head, slowly tracing the girl's skull, as if a line were being drawn with an invisible razor right before Nosipha's eyes. Droplets of blood flowed freely, and Jeli screamed from the pain. Nosipha cried.

The kingdom of the Snake. Black as those charred by the sun, hair of wool. His kingdom. In years to come, he would go on to unite both upper and lower Egypt. His name is Narmer Menes. His rule marked the first of written history. But he could not dismiss the roles of his griots. Everything has its place, and so, too, is that of the oral scribes. They must know the history and remember. Remember. It is a difficult and thankless job, but it must be done, as there are things said with the tongue that cannot be contained by writing, and there are things written that can never be spoken. So the griots held both the pen and the memory of an entire people.

Menes went on to rule for more than twenty years. He was a handsome man with thick lips and a wide, flat nose. He ruled with an iron fist but a soft heart. King Narmer was the first king to wear both the White Crown of Upper Egypt and Lower Egypt's Red Crown. The headdress was heavy and shaped like a round golden bowl. The king often bore scars from the crown.

He is your father; remember him, girl. Remember him.

Nosipha rushed her daughter to the hospital. Doctor Davidson arrived about a half hour after they did, because Nosipha had learned, in the many years she'd run back and forth to the emergency room, to call him on the way. Jeli's head had not stopped bleeding as the nurse unwrapped the makeshift bandage Nosipha had put on her daughter's head to soak up the drainage. The older woman, whose hands shook as she worked, commented that it looked like someone had placed an upside-down bowl around the girl's head and then tried to rip it off, skin and all. Doctor Davidson examined Jeli, looking over her very thoroughly, as he always did. But before he arrived, Jeli was examined by another doctor. The new man, Doctor Sanders, suspected Nosipha of wrongdoing. Nosipha had seen it before. Her daughter was prone to cuts and bruises in her condition, and over the years she'd been questioned on many occasions. The doctor questioned Nosipha about what had happened to the girl's head. Nosipha admitted, through tears, that she did not know. She told the man the wounds had simply appeared.

The doctor looked at her suspiciously, and she expected at any moment for him to call the authorities. Nosipha couldn't blame him for suspecting her of doing something to Jeli. Hell, if she didn't know better, she probably would have suspected herself, too. But what could she have done that would have caused this? So she explained that to this doctor, hoping he would understand that she was innocent.

"I'm not sure what you could have done. I understand things happen," the doctor responded. "Did you maybe wrap her head too tightly or something?"

"Something," she mocked him, "like what?" She realized he was trying to bait her. He wanted to catch her in a lie. "Why would I wrap her head up when it wasn't even bleeding in the first place? It doesn't make any sense."

"Well, you're the one telling us what happened, and I assure you it doesn't make any sense that the wound just appeared on her all of a sudden."

Nosipha was upset at the insinuation she'd done something to her daughter, even though she understood it. She'd done nothing but take care of Jeli night and day since the girl had been born. "Listen to me. I have bathed my daughter, cleaned her, fed her—many times through a tube when her sickness got too bad—and I have changed her diaper since the day she was born. I have never done anything to hurt her, and I will never harm my child. Do you understand me?" Tears began to stream from her eyes just as Doctor Davidson walked into the room.

Davidson took the other doctor out into the hall, and the two stayed outside talking for a long time. Nosipha was beginning to get worried; she knew this might not be a good sign. If they really thought she'd harmed her daughter, they would call the police on her and Jeli would be taken away and she could go to jail. If this happened, who would take care of Jeli? This was a nightmare. She thought back to what had happened. Yes, she was sure the girl had been lying in the bed, and as she convulsed, her body had gone stiff—and the marks had appeared. That was it. She knew it didn't make any sense, and she probably wouldn't believe it if she hadn't been there herself. But it was the truth and it was all she had.

She thought back to the day the girl had been born. Nosipha had been the happiest woman alive. She had wanted a baby for as long as she could remember. Nosipha hadn't been a young woman when the girl was born. The truth was, she'd been far past the recommended age to give birth at forty-two years old. But she could not have loved the girl any more if she'd been a young woman of twenty years, and that was what mattered.

As Jeli grew, Nosipha noticed she did not cry often. But she just assumed the girl was a good baby and she thanked God for this. Then Jeli would not crawl, and the girl didn't begin spouting those cute little baby mumblings as most babies do. It was obvious by the girl's first birthday, when the other children were smothering cake all over their faces and crawling around and getting into trouble, that something was very wrong. Jeli simply sat in her mother's arms pretending she didn't even notice the other children. There was something very different about her daughter, and at that point Nosipha had to stop pretending she didn't notice it.

Nosipha's grandmother told her to talk to the girl, telling her stories to make her feel as if she was a part of this world. But this was ridiculous; she spoke to her daughter all of the time. She sang to her and tried to teach her colors and numbers, but it just hadn't worked. This, her grandmother assured her, was not the same. Jeli had to *learn* things that had been lost to her, the old woman assured her. In fact, it had been lost to them both, her grandmother said, since Nosipha's mother had died when she was two, and she'd been raised by her father. She never even met her grandmother until she was almost twenty. Already in her declining years, Nosipha's grandmother alleged that she didn't remember what she had forgotten herself. In the end, the old woman died after Jeli was diagnosed, still forgetting what she could not remember, or at least forgetting to tell her granddaughter. Nosipha always regretted this; she always felt as if there was something she should have known, something she should, as her grandmother suggested, have taught her daughter.

After Nosipha noticed the problems with her daughter, she took the girl to the doctor. The doctor told her Jeli had a severe case of autism. He said Jeli had a "complete inability to communicate or interact with other people," and she would only get worse as the years passed.

It was true. The girl no longer even recognized Nosipha, her own mother, and she couldn't eat on her own; she had never used the toilet and she still couldn't walk or talk. Nosipha ran her fingers through her short kinky hair and sighed. Would things ever actually get better, or would they just continue getting worse? And worse and worse?

Doctor Davidson walked back into the room. He looked tired, and Nosipha knew if the man went through what he did with her for each of his patients, he should be ready to take a permanent nap. She knew she was.

"Everything's okay," the doctor said. "Doctor Sanders is just anxious and young. He doesn't understand this sickness."

"He thinks I did this, doesn't he? Is he calling the police?"

"No, no. He just didn't... I cleared everything up."

Nosipha stared at the doctor for a long time. Did he think she had done it?

He seemed to read her face. "Nosipha, I know you love Jeli. I know you couldn't hurt her. I am not going to pretend I know what happened here, but I'm confident you didn't do it." The man walked quietly out of the room, not looking back.

Movement behind the drawn white curtain caught her eye as the drape swung open. A woman with heavy dark circles around her eyes stared at Nosipha. Neither of the women spoke for a moment, letting the silence envelop the room. Finally, the woman whispered, her voice soft and fearful, "I couldn't help but hear. These damn sheets don't give you any privacy."

Nosipha nodded. "I'm sorry, I didn't even notice you were here." She glanced at her daughter sleeping quietly in her sterile white sheets, her skin ashen and dark. "I was just so...preoccupied, I guess."

The woman shrugged. "I can't blame you; I certainly understand." She pulled the sheet back to reveal a small, frail little boy swallowed within the covers. "Leukemia."

"I'm sorry."

"Not your fault. Not anyone's fault, I guess. It's just how it is." The women held out her hand so suddenly Nosipha almost jumped from the motion. "I'm Julia."

"I'm Nosipha." She shook the other woman's hand. "Nice to meet you. Maybe we can keep each other company in this dreadful place, huh?"

Just then the girl began to convulse in her bed. Her body contorted again into unimaginable angles, her fingers and toes crooked

39

and stiff. She didn't scream out, however, as her body threw itself from the bed and landed on the floor. Several nurses entered the room with the doctor, and they all helped get the girl back into bed. It wasn't an easy task; Jeli's body had become unbendable, like iron.

Girl, I am son of Sogolon and the Sun herself. I am Sundiata. I united the twelve kingdoms of ancient Mali by my iron sword. Those who knew me in life are all gone, as all people are subject to the laws of Heaven and Earth. And alas, kings are no different. I, however, get to take my place up in the sky with those who have come before me. We all know and remember. I remember the kingdoms, the wealth I acquired. I know the children of kings who served in my court. I remember the beautiful golden beads and silken treasures of wealth that I traded for slaves and concubines. Those of us who remember, do so because we must. Those who remember, remember because others have forgotten, and still others would steal our past. My dark skin. My memories. Those have been lost to history. They had been twisted to fit within an idea that does not represent what we truly were and who we have become. They... we must be remembered. You, my dear, must carry on. You must remember.

The girl awoke. As she lay in her bed, her head wrapped, blood seeping through the bandages, she screamed. Her mother thought she heard words within the scream. She'd said: *Son of...song...* something. But how could that be? Her daughter had not spoken a word in her entire twelve years of life. Nosipha didn't know if her daughter was even capable of speech after this much time. But there Jeli was, staring directly at her, her mouth forming as if she wanted to communicate with her mother for the first time ever. Nosipha desperately wished she knew what was happing to Jeli. What was happening to her daughter?

"What? What words?" The doctor stared at Nosipha as if he thought she was losing her mind. And now that she thought about it, Nosipha wasn't so sure that was not the case.

"I don't know. I just...thought maybe I heard her say something." Nosipha looked around for someone, anyone, to back her up, but Julia had gone out to get something to eat about a half hour before.

"Perhaps," Doctor Davidson placed his hands on her shoulders and squeezed, "maybe, it's simply wishful thinking on your part? Do you think this could be the case? Maybe?" He spoke to her as if she were a child.

She pulled away from him. "I know my daughter said something. I just don't..." She stared at the floor, almost ashamed to say anything further.

The doctor sighed, "What do you think she said?"

"Something like 'Son of son lay' or something like that. I'm not sure."

"And what does that mean?"

"I don't know."

"Well, my dear, if you don't understand them, then they're not words."

Nosipha walked back into her hospital room and slammed the door behind her. The doctor did not believe her daughter could possibly say anything. He, like everyone else, believed Jeli was just skin and bone; a lump of flesh incapable of human thought or emotion. But Nosipha knew better. She was sure she'd heard the girl. Doctor Davidson had said it might be time to consider putting Jeli in a home. He thought perhaps it was becoming too much for Nosipha to handle. He said he thought she was beginning to come apart and that he'd seen these signs many times before in parents in her situation. Nosipha simply stared at him, wondering if the doctor himself ever really saw his patients and their families at all. She thought perhaps the man only saw what he wanted to see. An autistic child who would never get better.

She turned to look at her daughter. Her child's eyes were moving rapidly under their lids, like she watched an invisible television screen within her sleep. The girl's frail body began to thrash and convulse again, and the tired woman who felt as if she'd grown older within the last two days whispered a silent prayer, *Please, God, not again.*

As the woman prayed, Jeli threw her legs over the rails of the bed, put there to protect the girl from herself. Then she sat up effortlessly, her back straight, erect. Julia walked over and placed her hand on Nosipha's shoulder, and the two watched in amazement, not sure what to do. Jeli had never sat up by herself before. Not on purpose, not like now. The girl opened her eyes and scanned the room again, this time focusing on her mother. This was impossible; Jeli couldn't see—not that well. Since the day she was born she couldn't focus on objects close to her face, certainly not anything across the room. The girl grabbed the rails of the bed—again on purpose—and swung herself over the edge. She landed on two very wobbly legs, her bare toes gripping the floor as they clenched tightly. Using the bedrail, and pure will power, Jeli headed for her mother. Her legs were so unsteady she almost fell, but she held on tightly just before her face smashed into the floor.

Nosipha realized what was happening before the girl fell again, and she caught her daughter just as she got to the end of the bed. The mother and daughter fell into each other, Nosipha crying loudly just as the doctor and nurse ran into the room.

"She walked."

Moments before, the girl had remembered:

> *He traveled from Mali to Egypt on his bare feet. When he grew tired, he rode on the backs of his many horses. But mostly he used the horses as mules to carry his great load. He brought gifts, as no king before him had. They say many years after his journey the effects of his gifts of gold could still be felt. His face was so clear to the girl this time.* She saw... *His words loud and clear in her head.* She knew... *He spoke to her; he was of her...her blood, her body, her spirit. Her very essence belonged to him and his people. She belonged to his story, which she realized was her story, too. Her mother's story, her mother's mother's story. They were the unremembered. And, he warned her, she could not forget. To forget would be to kill them all. To forget would be the death of a great people.*

"Why are you crying?" Nosipha asked Julia. "Is he okay? Is he doing poorly?"

The woman shook her head; her son had not gotten worse. She looked up at Nosipha, who slowly bent to hold her hand. "I'm mad at myself. I'm so jealous of you and your daughter. Jeli's getting better and Mario can't seem to keep food down. He's dying; I know it and the only thing I can think is why the hell can't it be my boy getting better. Why does my son have to die? I don't want to feel this way, but I can't help it. God, what a shitty person I must be, huh?"

Nosipha stared at the dying light piercing the window. "Jeli's not getting better; she's dying."

Father David came several days later. Nosipha felt a little ashamed to see him there. She had not been to church or paid her tithes in a long time. Hell, she couldn't even remember the last time she'd gone to church. She was surprised the priest even remembered her and her daughter. Then a thought came to her: maybe the man thought the girl was dying, so he had come to give her last rites. The thought scared Nosipha, but surprisingly, it relieved her more than she wanted to admit. Nosipha loved her daughter, but a person could only take so much. The man entered the room, looking around nervously as if he thought something waited in the shadows to grab him. The sight of Father David eased her mind a bit. She didn't pray often anymore, and she wasn't even sure she believed God cared about her or Jeli anymore. Maybe if this holy man was here supporting her, though, God wouldn't ignore her. He could not abandon her now.

"How is she?" the priest asked.

"They don't know. She took a step...but they don't know." Tears welled in the woman's eyes, and she wiped them away quickly.

The priest nodded.

The room fell silent and Nosipha felt as if the man wanted more. "I haven't been to church in a while, I know. But it hasn't been easy. I... I've had a lot..."

"We understand. It has to be hard taking care of a child like this by yourself. Expensive. The church sympathizes." He walked over to the girl and touched the bandages around her head. "They tell me she bled around the crown of her head. What happened?"

"I don't know. One minute she was fine and the next, she was bleeding."

"Did you see it appear?"

"Yeah, it just...happened. I didn't do anything to her."

"Have you been praying, Sister? Prayed with Jeli?"

Nosipha shrugged her shoulders, hung her head in shame. "Maybe not as much as I should. I know... I... I should have done more. Maybe..."

"Maybe, my dear. He still listens and understands your suffering and pain."

This revelation made the woman cry even more. *He heard and understood her pain.* Father David put his arms around her. She felt better, comforted. "What are the doctors saying, my dear?"

She wiped her face. "They don't know. They think it may be her last hurrah, or something, I don't know. They said her muscles can't just get stronger so they may actually be...fading. I think they think she's dying."

He lifted her face toward him. "And what do you think?"

"I don't know what to think."

"You want to know what I think?" She nodded; she did want to know what he thought, she desperately wanted to know. "I think God has chosen this child. And now I think the church could help her to bring a lot of people to Him."

While Father David discussed important matters with Nosipha, the nurses checked Mario, Julia's son. The boy stopped breathing and the doctors revived him after a very dramatic couple of seconds. Nosipha stood by the woman, holding her hand, trying to ease pain her a bit. But Nosipha knew there was no way to ease this pain. Just to think about the loss of a child was unbearable, and to actually watch one die was inconceivable. The woman held onto her as if the two had been the best of friends all their lives—they shared secrets. Luckily, the doctors revived Mario and the boy's vitals were close to normal again. Julia didn't seem to trust this, though, as she kept checking the boy to make sure he was okay. Nosipha heard the doctors tell Julia she might want to consider a Do Not Resuscitate order since it had happened several times now. Julia yelled for the men to get out, not wanting to accept it.

The priest held Nosipha's hand, assuring her everything would be all right.

In the bed beside them, Jeli slowly raised up and turned her head to face her mother and the priest. Nosipha, her back to the bed, followed the man's gaze until she saw her daughter sitting upright, staring into the distance. Jeli did not see her mother because her eyes were as black as coal, blacker than the girl's skin. They looked like tiny jewels stuck into her head. Jeli opened her mouth to speak, but nothing came out. She moved her lips as if she were holding a conversation the others were not privy to. Then she let out a long, low moan. Nosipha rose to her feet, getting ready to go to her daughter, and the priest stopped her. "Just wait," the man said.

But Jeli did not wait. She threw her head back and let out the loudest scream she could muster. She had not spoken in over a decade, and her vocal cords seemed to be developing in her throat. Her cry was mangled and strange, the octaves wavering up and down like a person with laryngitis. Nosipha could not believe it; she didn't know what to do. She wanted to run out to get a doctor, but she didn't want to leave her daughter. So she stayed and watched.

The girl's black eyes seemed to look straight through everyone. She felt a strange sensation take over her body without knowing fully that this indeed was her body. She wasn't even sure what part of her feelings were directly related, or what parts she simply imagined as she had for the past twelve years. Her head whirled and spun with images she knew to be real, but that she could not distinguish from past or present. On some level she knew who she was; she had known it, she believed, all along. But now she knew other things, important things, powerful things. And, as she knew now, knowledge is power.

The knowledge she saw was telling. Images darted in and out of her head so fast she could no longer keep up with them. But she no longer tried. She let them run over her like a waterfall. This, too, had the same effect: it was calming, cooling. Now she simply accepted what she saw and knew to be truth.

> *Tall white men on tall white horses come to trade, they say, to learn…they create powerful Gods in their honor… pain, darkness, suffering…people being ripped from their homes, their masters… Remember…long voyages, desolate damp deathful spaces…the…church…acceptance… condoning…facilitating… Remember…dark babies dying by*

their own mothers hands to protect them from barring the bonds of... Remember...*money...power...* Remember... them... Remember us all. *The slavery, my dear, was not the most difficult part; no, the hard part was the loss. The loss of everything past, present and future. To take away one's past is to deny them a future.*

The girl shook her head, not sure she could take any more. It was overpowering. How could anyone carry this much on her shoulders? She'd been in the dark for so long, her mind cluttered, not remembering her name, much less where she came from or what she had been meant to do. *Her great grandmother...* That's right. She remembered the old woman had spoken to her also, telling her what her mother, Nosipha, had forgotten. Her great grandmother remembered until she'd gotten too old to pass it on, and then she died. But she died before she could teach the knowledge. Jeli's mother was too old then, and by the time Jeli was born it was too late, the knowledge was lost, leaving her a shell of who she should have been.

But not anymore.

Jeli's body buckled, a spasm taking over again. Her arms flailed, throwing her body all over the bed. When she reached the edge, the girl threw herself over the side and hit the floor with a loud bang.

Julia gasped and ran over to the girl's side. Nosipha and Father David joined her, and the two women knelt down by the girl's side, checking for any sign of life. Beside Nosipha, the priest crossed himself and said a silent prayer. At that moment, Jeli's eyes flew open, the whites clearly visible now.

Everyone in the room jumped, giving the girl a wide berth. Slowly, as if being pulled by a rope connected to a plank, Jeli rose to her feet in one fluid motion. The girl's eyes were clear; so was her mind. She could see and think clearly for the first time in her short life. As she stared around the room, she focused on each person, one at a time. Finally, she stepped forward on two wobbly legs. At first her mother didn't think she would make it, but with each step, the girl's legs got stronger. Her face had changed, too. She looked older, as if she'd aged with years of wisdom of a woman many years her senior.

The girl walked toward Father David and he smiled, his arms outstretched, waiting to embrace her. The man was proud, as if he not only had witnessed this miracle, but as if he owned it. Slowly, assuredly, Jeli walked past him, toward the child sleeping quietly in the next bed. She placed her hand on Mario. Fingers that once could not uncurl themselves to hold a fork now moved gracefully over Mario's flesh. The boy opened his eyes, smiled up at Jeli. She leaned down and whispered something to him the others could not hear. Slowly, the boy's color seemed to darken a bit. His ashen brown face began clear into a deep, dark tone. Julia jumped to her feet and ran to her son.

When she was finished, Jeli turned to her mother and the other man. She looked at him, her eyes fixed. The man stared, as if a child waiting for recognition from a parent.

"What you want from me, I cannot give. I've been shown the knowledge of the past. And since you can't use me, you will seek to discredit me. Much like your Savior. But I know the truth." The priest suddenly averted his eyes, as if lost or afraid of the girl's glare. Jeli tilted her head, faced the priest, and whispered so softly her mother was not sure she heard the girl properly. Then she said simply, "Because I remember."

The man got to his feet, straightened his suit coat, and quietly walked out of the room, knowing, if nothing else, that he would not be adding this soul to his flock.

"CHOCOLATE PARK"

Ebony walked through the park alone. The night around her seemed to make her dark skin invisible. The path narrowed, forked and split off into two directions, the right darker than the left. She took the right.

She did not hesitate, as she knew exactly where she was headed. She had been there before. She'd left behind all the street lamps long ago, all signs of civilization. Only night was ahead. The branches of the nearby trees shook and arched, as if arms, warning her away.

She tripped over a tree stump that had split straight through the sidewalk, stood, dusted herself off, and walked on. To the right, just past the shadows, she heard a rustling sound in the bushes. She walked toward it.

A loud scream broke the silence, and she jumped despite herself.

But she knew that voice.

She rounded the bend, past the large oak, and saw them. Two forms lying naked under the blanket of night. Another scream erupted, and Ebony realized that this was a shout of pleasure, not pain.

"Coco!" Ebony called.

The man jumped, surprised by her presence. By anyone's presence. This park should have been deserted at this time of night. And, except for the three of them, it just may have been. Only the drunks and junkies dared to roam these woods after dark.

He sat up and looked at her, angry.

Ebony noticed him right away: one of the local dealers, Torch. He was known for burning the skin off junkies who owed him money, with a cigarette lighter. Loved the smell, they said. She didn't care. She had come this far for her sister, and she wouldn't leave without her.

"Coco," she said, her words bouncing off the trees and back into her ears, "get up from there."

The girl didn't answer.

"Get up. We're going home."

"I ain't goin' nowhere," Ebony's sister said. Beneath the dark man, her body was almost invisible.

"Get up, damn it!"

"She ain't goin' nowhere, girl, 'til I get my money's worth. Now get." The man lay back down and began pumping her sister. Ebony walked over to them and pushed him off. "Keep your filthy hands off my sister."

"Your sister seems filthy enough on her own. You shoulda' been here a minute ago when she was suckin' my dick." He laughed.

Coco stood up without modesty, breasts and pubic hair visible in the moonlight.

"Get outta here, Eb."

"Yeah," Torch agreed. "Before we make this a threesome. You ever done it before, li'l girl?"

Coco stepped between him and her sister. "She ain't no ho. I'll take care of you."

"Well, maybe things have changed." He caressed his genital area. "Come on, let me show you what a real man can do."

"No." Coco said.

"Let's go." Ebony grabbed her arm.

"Oh no you don't!" Torch rushed at Coco, pushing her to the ground. She fell face forward in the grass. He kicked her in the stomach; she gagged, caught her breath, and coughed. "You stupid trick bitch." He kicked her again.

He ran toward Ebony. His angry eyes and teeth protruding through a wicked smile were the only things she could see through the darkness. Those were enough.

He was going to hurt her. Bad.

He stopped when he saw the silver pistol in her hands, aimed at his head.

"You don't know how to use that piece, li'l girl. Now put it down before I bash your head in with it." He took a step closer.

"Don't come no closer, man. I'll shoot you, I swear it."

"No you won't." He laughed.

On the ground, Coco sat up and looked at Ebony. "Where the hell did you get that thing, Eb?"

Ebony spoke, not taking her eyes off Torch, the barrel still aimed at his face, "You think I learned nothin' from Momma, when she used to come out at night lookin' for you? I know where she kept it."

"Put it away—you'll hurt someone." Coco stood up, holding her stomach.

"Not if he just lets us walk away."

"Hell no!" Torch shook his head. "I paid her for it, now she's gotta deliver. She took my stuff. Tell her to put the gun down, Chocolate."

"I'll pay," Coco said.

"No you won't. Give him the stuff back."

"I can't. It's... It's gone."

Ebony glanced at her older sister just long enough for her to see the anger in her eyes. "You doin' drugs again, Coco? Who am I kiddin'? Of course you are." She tipped the gun on its side, still pointing the barrel toward Torch. She switched off the safety. "Now you can either let us go, or I can shoot you. Right here where you stand. You know they won't find the body for days, and then they'll just think another dealer did it. So what ya think? Say?"

He stood there for a moment as if contemplating his options, staring into Ebony's eyes. When she did not waver, he bent down and scooped up his clothes.

"This shit ain't over, bitch," he said, stepping into his shoes. "I'll burn my money out of your ass, if I have to."

At eighteen years old, Ebony had already taken on the role of mother to her fourteen-year-old sister, Sable. As well as Coco, who, at twenty, had been a prostituting drug addict even before their mother had died when she was seventeen. They had no father to speak of, so none of them did. No one else to count on, except each other. And most of the time, they couldn't count Coco, so there was only the two.

Ebony had already gotten Sable off to school and done the breakfast dishes before it was time to go to work at the phone company. She had gotten the job through a friend of her mother's and had worked there a little over six months. It paid most of the bills; anything she couldn't pay for just got shut off.

On the way out the door, Ebony ran into Lady Black. Everyone in the neighborhood called her that because she was more proper and pleasant than most in that part. Her easygoing way called for respect, despite the fact that she was still black, like the rest of them. The main reason, Ebony thought, that they called the old woman

Lady Black was because she was known to dabble in Black Magic. Ebony had seen no evidence of this, though.

The old woman always told Sable stories of how things had been in the neighborhood when she had been younger. Sable loved the Lady, and Ebony imagined that the Lady felt the same for her sister. If she had to admit it, she would have said that the Lady scared her more than anything. It was her eyes.

"Well, there, how is the most important part of the Three Musketeers?" She always called Ebony that.

"Off to work. Someone has to pay the bills." She smiled.

"Too bad it's you, huh?" The old lady's eyes had a way of saying much more than her mouth, and Ebony found herself turning away. Those eyes had said too much. Ebony shrugged.

"Where would the Miss be right now, if she had her choice?"

"Oh, boy." Ebony closed her eyes, letting the thought take her where it would. She opened them, a sad look on her face. "Where else could I go? Coco and Sable need me."

The old woman stared at her in surprise, as if she had never heard such nonsense in her life. "Why, anywhere you want, girl. Anywhere in the world."

When she left the old woman, she saw the old man from upstairs. He wasn't really old like Lady Black. About thirty-five, Ebony guessed. She had come to call him that because he made it a habit to chase girls much younger than himself. The younger the better. Ebony had even caught him flirting with Sable. She hated him.

"I saw your sister Chocolate gettin' in some old man's car. You think she was gonna do him?"

Pervert, she thought. "Her name's Coco."

"Well, they call her Chocolate on the streets."

"Not all of us hang out in the street." She didn't even bother smiling; he knew she despised him.

"Well," he did smile, showing all of his toothless gums, "some of us make it our job to *work* the streets."

"My sister's not a whore," she yelled.

"Maybe you should tell *her* that." He smiled at her one more time before he walked away.

Perhaps she should talk to Lady Black. Find out if there was any truth to the rumor. She smiled at the thought.

On the bus ride to work, Ebony sat quietly and alone. It

seemed that was the way she spent most of her time, lately. When she was at home, Coco was never there, and Sable was usually at school. Secretly, she longed for more, but she didn't quite know what to do about it. How could she leave the only home she had ever known? Coco would never go. She considered this her home. And it was home. To all of them. Mamma had lived and died here. Perhaps they all would as well.

Time goes by slowly in the projects. Most of the time it seems to stop completely.

No money.

No job.

No hope for the future; no reason for time.

Ebony worked her job at the phone company. Coco—a.k.a. Chocolate—worked her corner. But most importantly, her job was to find her next fix. Sable had just turned fifteen and had a longing to go to college. Ebony actually thought she could make it, on a scholarship with her 3.8 GPA.

She was proud. She wanted Sable to have more than she had. She wanted her to become more than just a junkie like Coco. Or a phone rep, like her.

"You really think I can?" Sable asked, sitting at the table finishing up her homework.

"Of course you can. I've told you that."

Sable twirled around, hands held high in the air, almost lost in thought. "Maybe I'll be a doctor. Get an office on the south side here. Help some of us without insurance and money. What ya think? I could, right?"

"Yeah." Ebony smiled.

"But..." She drifted off as if she had heard a voice in the back of her head, telling her not to say anymore.

"But what?"

"Coco said that ain't nobody in this family never been to college and neither would I."

"She said that?"

"Yeah." Sable paused, and Ebony saw the hurt in her eyes. "You know she ain't been home in two days?"

Ebony nodded her head. "I know."

"You gonna go get her? Can I come too?"

"No! I'll do this alone." Ebony allowed a single tear to fall down her sullen face.

"Momma used to cry too," Sable whispered.

Ebony didn't hear.

She found Coco in the park again. She wasn't surprised. The surprise was that she was alone.

"Let's go home, Co."

"Did you bring your gun this time, Officer?"

"I never know what I'm gonna find you with. Momma told me that. She told me to take care of you. Who is it nowadays? Anyone who pays, right? You'll fuck anyone who pays!"

"Right!" Coco screamed, wobbled forward, and fell to the ground.

Ebony could tell she was high. Crack. "So you can buy that shit. Why?"

"Because..." She stood up and brushed invisible dirt stains from her knees, like a pro.

"Because what, Coco?"

"It's Chocolate to you. To everyone! My name's Chocolate."

"Let's go home now." She reached out to her sister.

Coco slapped her hand away. "I am home. Don't you see?" She twirled in a circle, her arms outstretched. She fell again, then stood up. "Home. This is Chocolate Park. My park. My home."

Ebony looked at her sister and began to cry. She knew that Coco had been doing drugs for a long time. She even knew about the prostituting, despite denying it. But she had never seen her like this. Maybe, she realized, she had never allowed herself to see it. She loved her, damn it. She did.

Coco had taken it hard when she found out their mother had cancer. She had felt responsible, as if she hadn't been there for their mother when she had needed her the most. And of course she hadn't been, because of the drugs. Then, when she died, Coco had been stuck with all the responsibilities of two younger sisters. Motherhood. But hell, so had Ebony. The only difference was that Ebony was good at it.

"Do you want to join me?" Chocolate said. Ebony did not see her as Coco any longer; her sister had died. "I can help you. You know, show you the ropes. Even help you find johns. What ya think? All in the family."

Ebony wiped her eyes. "Sable ran into Torch today. He said he wants his money or his stuff. He said he'd kill you to get it. He said he'd kill her, too. Do you care?"

The drugs wouldn't let her.

The day Torch raped Sable, she had been walking home from school and he'd grabbed her and pulled her into his car.

He drove her to his apartment, and one by one, he and his buddies had their way with her.

When he sent her to walk home, he told her, "Tell Chocolate, I want my money. Or next time I'll kill you, bitch." And... "You even think about goin' to the FOLKS—*the cops*—and my boys will kill all three of you."

How do you choose one sister over the other?

Ebony got the call at work. Her sister was hurt. Sable had gone to Lady Black's apartment; their phone had been long since disconnected.

When Ebony walked in, she saw her. Sable's eyes were swollen shut and had a deep cut in one lid. Torch had knocked out one of her teeth, and it had lodged in her lip so the girl could barely talk. The right side of her face was completely bruised, and she had small circular burn marks on her face and body. Ebony could tell that Sable had been crying, but now she put on a brave—even strong—face for her sister.

Ebony couldn't do the same; she cried. "Oh my God. What did he do to you?"

Sable sat up on the couch. "He didn't do this." The pain from her embedded tooth was obvious.

"You mean, Torch didn't...?"

"Oh yeah, he did it with his buddies." She covered her mouth as blood poured from her lips. "But Co, she let it happen. She's been hurting us for a long time. This is just another way."

How do you choose one sister over the other? Ebony looked at Lady Black, whose eyes once again told her everything she needed to know. Louder than words they shouted:

"Pack your stuff; we're leavin'. *Now!*"

Ebony found Coco in Chocolate Park with her john. "Get up

and leave. Now!" she told the man.

He looked at her strangely, but didn't argue. He stood up, zipped his pants, and ran off.

Chocolate just lay there, naked.

"Torch wants his money." Ebony said.

"I'll pay. I'll pay, okay?"

"When?"

"When I can."

"He raped Sable. Him and his fucking friends. They raped her."

"What?" To Ebony's surprise, she looked concerned. "He what?"

"Beat her up too. Bad."

Chocolate covered her face. She cried, Ebony could see her tears glisten in the moonlight. But Ebony felt no remorse.

"How much stuff is worth him raping Sable? Huh, Chocolate? How much?"

She sobbed. "I stole some of his stash. I was gonna pay it back, I swear."

"When?"

"When did I take it? A couple of weeks ago. I didn't even think he'd notice. I... I was gonna pay him back."

Ebony shook her head. "You fuckin' junkie. What you gonna do about it?"

"Do? What can I do?"

"I don't know. Do something to keep him from hurting Sable again."

"He'll kill me!" she cried.

"He raped your sister. Isn't that enough? And I know that's why you haven't been home—so he couldn't find you. You've been hiding out. But if you go to him, tell him you'll pay, maybe..."

"I... I can't."

"He said he'd kill her next time. He said he'd kill her, Chocolate!"

"I can't."

Ebony shook her head. "I knew it. You're a coward. You won't even do it to help Sable." She sighed. "I expected as such. Well, I'm taking her and leaving. Getting outta this stinkin' shit-hole. Come with us, Co. Come with u—"

The shot came from behind Ebony. It echoed, bouncing from tree to tree.

Instinctively, she ducked and fell to the ground. When she looked up, the second shot pierced Chocolate's chest. The first had hit her in the stomach.

Ebony looked at the shooter.

Sable.

The girl cried and dropped the gun. "We don't need her, Eb. Momma use to cry. Did you know that? I would hear her through the walls. She would cry. She'd cry for her. Now she's made you cry, too. And me." She wiped her eyes. "But we don't have to cry for her anymore. We can forget her. The drugs had her anyway."

In the end, the choice was easy. Choosing one sister over the other.

The hard part was burying Coco in her Chocolate Park.

2

Lady Black, whose real name was Dieula-Marie Balan, which means "God is here," had lived in Bowen Homes for more than half of her sixty-nine years. She had seen things change for the better with integration and then for the worse when drugs came on the scene—but as far as she was concerned, it was all the same. This had only been for the last ten or fifteen years or so, but that had been long enough to change the lives of the people around her.

She had seen how that demon had transformed the young girl from downstairs. They had been good girls. And she had seen how her own son, Jacob, had become another victim of its power. Her son had been a good kid. Just as Coco had been.

She closed her eyes, not wanting the memory of Jacob to invade her senses as it usually did. A tear still managed to fall down her dark jaw. She wiped it away quickly and smoothed her wild white mane of hair. Outside, the sun was setting, which left the room in a vivid orange hue.

Lady walked over to the makeshift broom closet off the front hall and pulled back the bedspread hung as a curtain, which was there to replace the missing door. The humble room was little more than a pantry, but it held a special place in the Lady's black heart.

She struck the match with the extra-long stem and lit all of the extra-long red candles surrounding her bowl of special herbs, crushed to a fine powder. On her knees, she glanced at each of the dolls that adorned her faded white walls, each representing a person in her life, and assured herself that all of their positions remained the same as she had placed them. Indeed, they did.

Lady Black had been practicing black magic for most of her life. Originally from Haiti, she worshiped the fine art and used it wisely. She knew things. Certain things that most didn't know—or cared not to. She knew of the dark side and used it to her advantage. She knew of the old and the new, the strong and frail. Death. She did not mind giving to the dark side, if in the end, it would give back to her. And she knew without doubt that it would.

The air hung heavy in the modest apartment, stale and cold. The way she liked it.

But everything was not quiet; next door the young couple in apartment 4B started arguing again. He screamed and banged on the walls, as always, and she cried and clung to their screaming child. The Lady did not have to see this, in her apartment only a wall away from the young couple, to know it.

"Someone must put a stop to that one day," she shouted, though she knew that they would never hear her above their own destructiveness.

As the young man next door punched the wall again and threatened his wife with an outburst of profanity, sending a frame of Lady's dead son crashing to the floor, she slapped the wall with an open hand and shouted to him, "Stop the drama!"

The walls were thin in this place. Not suited to house rats. But it did—rats and people. The housing projects—where you could get in, but getting out was a son-of-a-bitch.

The thin walls hadn't always seemed so bad, though. When she had first moved here almost fifty years ago, she didn't remember having to put up with the screaming matches of her overworked neighbors. Or the love-making of the overworked rabbits in the upstairs apartment—the one with half a dozen kids. Perhaps, over the years, like most things, the walls had aged. Thinned. Worn by the day-to-day endlessness of their own existence.

Perhaps.

Lady threw on her cape and headed out the door. The next-door couple was beginning to get out of hand, and she needed some fresh air. Not to mention bread and milk. In the halls, the fresh scent of urine and sweat hit her. Musty sweat, evidence of long, hard workdays for very little money.

Descending the stairs one step at a time—she didn't get around so good anymore—she saw another of the resident rats, Fast Charley. He had gotten that name because he was a fast talker—could worm himself out of a jam, and in fact, had done so on many occasions—and even faster with the ladies. Although the only "ladies" Lady Black had seen him with were young enough to be his daughters.

Fast Charley had one hand propped against the wall, still fondling a cigarette as the ash grew longer than the butt, and the other blocking some young girl's way. He kept her there with the weight of his bony body as he whispered something, no doubt filthy, into the girl's ear. As she got closer she realized who the girl was.

Sable. One of the Three Musketeers from the second floor— her favorite Musketeer.

"Hey you," Lady Black yelled. The man startled, as if caught doing something wrong, and dropped his arm to his side. "You leave that girl alone."

Charley looked up and seemed relieved that it was only the old woman. "Mind your own business, ol' witch." He had called her that since he had moved in a little over a year ago. Everyone in the building knew she dabbled in the fine art of black magic. In fact, most had come to her to right a wrong that they felt had been done to them at one point or another.

She liked it that way; she liked to help people.

Not Fast Charley. He seemed to get off on making her angry. He would taunt her and call her a witch at every chance he got. She hated him.

"Listen, you little runt, you leave that girl alone or I'll turn that pecker of yours into a peanut with one snip, you hear?" She moved her fingers in scissor motions as she smiled at the thought.

He stepped back away from Sable, who took the opportunity to dash up the stairs. "Look what you did." He tried to act like he hadn't heard her last comment.

"Stay away from her, Charley," she said. She stared at him with eyes that, at least to Charley, seemed to shimmer blood red and then back to black. Only she knew that, in fact, they had.

"Mind your own business, ol' woman." Again, he pretended not to notice.

He had. She was sure of it. He flicked his cigarette to the floor and walked past her, not bothering to stomp it out. She hated that.

She bent down, picked up the butt, and snuffed it out with her thumb and forefinger. She put the butt in her pocket.

At Sam's Market, she bought milk, eggs, fish and bread (they were having a two for one sale). Lady had never really learned to read—she had only made it to the second grade in school, despite the well-educated tone in her voice—but she had figured out enough to get by. She cut coupons from the paper and even brought them on occasion. Mostly she only read the pictures, though. *A picture's worth a thousand words,* she'd heard that somewhere once. It seemed true enough to her now.

Outside Sam's she saw him. He was standing at the corner, pushing some of his poison to one of the kids who lived in the next building over from hers.

Eddie Roberts scanned his surroundings, not seeing her, handed the young man his package with a quick, cupped hand, got the money, and walked away. All in fifteen seconds or so. Pretty good. He had become an expert over the years.

Eddie walked toward her; he didn't see her until he was right on her.

He stopped. Stared.

Eddie hadn't changed much since she had seen him the first time in over ten years before. "What ya starin' at, ol' woman? Ain't ya seen enough of me in all these years?" He didn't smile.

He knew better.

Lady Black, who had not gotten that name until many years later, had first met Eddie Roberts in 1989 when her son Jacob had brought him home. She had to admit that she didn't like him any more now than she had then. Eddie had befriended her son. Protected him from the bullies at school, got him to sell drugs for him, and then gotten him hooked on the drugs he sold, all in less than a year's time.

Then Eddie had shot Jacob in the head and torched his body for using the drugs he should have sold. Of course, no one was ever able to link him to the murder, and Eddie denied everything. But she was sure it was him. Hell, his street name told it all.

Torch.

As far as she was concerned, Eddie had murdered her boy. She could not prove it, but that didn't stop her from calling the police every chance she got. To no avail, of course. She wanted him to rot in jail, which would be the worst punishment a man like him could get. She would revenge her son, though; she was sure of it as she stood and stared at this monster.

She looked at the man who towered more than a foot over her, and she smiled.

An evil smile.

The smile of a thousand Black Ladies; the smile that every Lady before her had smiled; her mother's mother's smile from somewhere within the depths of her soul. It said, *somehow, someplace, I'm coming for you.*

Torch saw no blood; he saw no red in her eyes, as she didn't allow it, but he dashed away just as fast as Charley had.

He had seen much more.

Darkness greeted her in her tiny one bedroom apartment. She did not mind. She had found that she liked that.

Peace also awaited her; the couple from next door had quieted down. Not even the baby cried.

That was strange. He always cried.

The police siren came next.

The next day the girl, Sable, came over after school. This was not unusual; she always dropped by to see her. The Lady loved Sable very much.

"And to what do I owe the pleasure of this visit, my dear?"

Sable laughed. She had a beautiful laugh. "Does a friend need a reason to visit a...friend?" They had rehearsed this line often.

Lady let the girl in. "Co's been gone for two nights," Sable said.

"I know."

The girl looked at her strangely, as if she had used some form of magic to see in her mind. It was nothing as grand as that. "I usually hear her drag herself in at night. After..." she didn't want to say more "...after she gets home," she lied.

"After she's done hoin'," Sable said.

"Don't talk that way 'bout your sister."

"Why not? She doesn't care about us. No more than she cared about Momma."

Lady Black was speechless for the first time since her son had died. The girl was right. The only thing her sister cared about was the drugs she used to get her quick fix. But she understood more than Sable that her sister was a slave to the drugs and couldn't control herself any more than Sable could control hating her.

"You don't have to say anything, Lady. Just like Momma. She used to cry, ya know? At night, when she thought no one could hear."

"I know." She *had* used her abilities when she had heard the girl's mother crying. However, anyone with their ears open to it could have heard that woman's weep. It was embedded in the building's thin walls. Lots of suffering was there.

The lady felt it; anyone who set foot in that door felt it. They were part of it.

"I know you know, Lady." The girl hugged her and they both melted into one another as if by the heat of the sun.

The next time she saw Sable, the girl was different. It was only a week later, after school, but she had changed.

She had been raped. Spoiled. Changed.

"Oh my God, child! What happened to you?" The girl mumbled something, but the Lady just blocked it out.

Shock.

The girl's face was swollen. Her eye was black and bruised shut. When she tried to speak, the blood gurgled in her mouth. She had dozens of circular marks on her face and arms. Burns. Probably from a cigarette. Some of them were already blistering, full of puss.

"Oh, my baby."

Lady Black tried to help Sable to the couch, but she fell several feet short. Her hands, all cut and torn, searched the carpet as she tried to pull herself up.

"Sable?"

The fifteen-year-old girl, whose one goal in life had been to become a doctor to help people, had been tortured. Tormented.

"Torch..." she heard the girl say. "He...raped me." Tears ran down Sable's face, and the Lady joined the young girl on the floor. Her old bones creaked in pain, but she ignored them. Her Musketeer was hurting.

She cradled Sable in her arms. "I'll call Eb. She'll know what to do."

When Ebony left with Sable, she had known that she would never see either girl again.

She preferred it that way. They would be able to make a better life outside of this hellhole, without the pain and without Coco.

The Lady had seen in Sable's eyes what the girl had planned to do.

And she agreed. Sometimes debts had to be repaid.

Most people assume that black magic is some kind of demonic force or something that is only in the magician's head. But this is not true. The truth is that if the person is strong enough, the power that is transferred can be excruciating.

And Lady Black was strong.

She took the little yellow doll from the wall—yellow for coward—and placed the cigarette from her pocket into the hole in the doll's face she had carved for the mouth. She had already moistened the butt, ensuring that the saliva would cling to the fabric.

She removed the doll's clothes, as hers were removed. It was completely anatomically correct; she was glad for that now.

Pain was not her mission, but she didn't need to worry; this would be insufferable.

Her experience had taught her that.

She chanted a few key words, only for effect now, only habit. Her power was strong enough that she didn't need them anymore. But it eased her mind to speak them out loud. It comforted her. She was a creature of habit, and habit created peace for the Lady.

Lady Black closed her eyes and repeated the chant thrice and asked for the blessing of the spirits of the underground. The ones that owed her favors. And the ones she planned to repay later.

She took out the only ingredient she needed for this incantation to work: lye. The smell was strong and hung heavier in the room than the candle smoke.

As soon as she dipped the doll's pecker into the potent potion, she heard the scream. Although almost inaudible in this never-ending torment of pain and suffering of the place that she called home, she still recognized it.

Fast Charley.

She smiled.

She knew that the plague would begin in his genitals, burning and itching and becoming black as ash, and within hours, would spread to the rest of his body.

This time there would be no police.

3

They usually argued over simple things, like most couples do—the bills, the housework, sex—but this time was different. It was vicious. They say sometimes that if you drop a pin during the middle of an argument you will lose it—the pin and the argument. However, right now, David was sure that he would not only lose the pin and the fight, but his mind as well.

"It's getting too fucking late and I have to work the night shift. I need some sleep."

"We all need sleep, David." Angie clung to their three-month-old child as if he were going to jump right out of her arms.

The baby cried. He always cried. This was nothing new.

David and Angie had been high school sweethearts. Angie had become pregnant two months before they'd graduated, and now, within a year's time, they were married, had a kid, and were trying to manage everything on his two full-time jobs. They had been forced to move to the projects because neither of their parents would allow them to live with them, not that they had come from particularly well-to-do families anyway. At first, they had felt strange because they were the only white family in the building, but the neighbors had welcomed them.

It was hard. His parents and teachers had tried to tell him to go to college and wait on the family. But the family was already made, and he felt that he could not abandon them. He *would not* abandon them.

That was then. Now he just wanted to run as far and as fast as he could get on the seventy-five dollars that he had in his pocket. Courtesy of Morgan Frot, the meanest asshole to ever run a meat house.

The baby began to choke on his spit, stopped crying, and then resumed full force again.

"God, can't you just shut him up?" David yelled.

"How? He has colic. He will stop—"

"When? When, huh? When will he shut up? Just about the time that I have to go to fucking work?"

Angie began to sniff. "He can't help it." Then the tears began.

She stood only two feet away from him, and he wanted to reach out and slap her face. But he couldn't do that. Could he? No, probably not, she would call the police, hell, probably even his mother. Lord knows she had called his parents before when they had got into it.

"Oh, don't you fucking cry. Don't you dare. I can't take it; you and the kid."

She did anyway.

David swept his hands thought his hair and pulled. The pressure from the pull was minor and did not abate his frustration. "Fuck!" He ran over to the wall and kicked it. But that did not satisfy his need to hit someone. So, he put his fist through the plaster wall of their tiny one bedroom apartment. It went straight through, almost right into the other side, he thought. Stinging hot pain ran up his arm to his chest and he fell to his knees in protest.

Angie gasped.

Blood ran down his knuckles, and he was relieved to have felt the pain. To have felt anything in this house. He had not had feelings for Angie in a long time—hell, since the baby had come. They had not even made love since her third trimester, and he was happy for that. Angie did not get the urges anymore, and he no longer found her attractive. She had put on almost fifty pounds. She looked like a cow. She didn't even try to lose the weight, either. She just sat in front of the tv all day and ate.

Cow.

She walked over to him. "Are you all right?"

"Don't fucking touch me." He pulled away from her.

The baby stopped crying. Angie did not.

The neighbor pounded on the wall and it rang throughout the apartment. "Hey over there," the woman yelled, "stop the drama."

The baby cried again.

"Fuck!" David jumped to his feet, holding his bloodied left hand. He kicked the wall again. "Fuck you, asshole."

"David, just calm down," Angie yelled, tears staining her two-day-old shirt.

"Calm down? You and that goddamn kid are driving me crazy. You sit here all day while I'm out busting my ass. And that kid waits just for the moment that I get home to cut up. And you want me to calm down!"

"I don't just sit here all day and do nothing, David. I know you don't believe me, but it's hard work taking care of him. I do my best. I try to keep him quiet but he can't help it. He's colicky."

He looked at his wife and at the child in her arms, and at that moment he hated them both. "He can't help it? I work all fucking day, and he can't just shut the hell up when I get home." Anger had replaced his drowsiness, and he just wanted it all over. He wanted them gone; the baby, the wife, and the responsibility.

"You can't shut him up," he ran toward her, "I will."

She ran away. She had every right to be afraid; he did not know what he planned to do when he caught them—he hadn't really thought about it—but he knew it would not be good. She made it as far as the other side of the room when she stopped and fell back into the wall. Probably afraid to run anymore; afraid of him.

He did not stop to grab her; he walked past her into the kitchen. He paused for a moment, looked around, and went straight for the knife drawer. His parents had given them a large cutlery set for a wedding gift. Now he was glad for it. He took out the biggest, sharpest knife he could find.

A fucking monster, it was. He caressed the blade with his good hand, while holding the butt with his bad one. Then he switched the handle to his good one; he felt it, twirling it and slicing the air to get a feel for it. "Oh, yes, this will do fine." He returned to the room with his two mistakes.

Stop the drama, the scary old woman from next door had yelled.

"Stop the drama. I'll stop it right now." His parents and his teachers had warned him. But he had not listened.

Angie began to cry again when she saw the knife. She stood up and put the baby on the floor behind her, shielding him from his father.

"What are you doing, David?" the tears were gone; only the desire to survive remained.

"I can't do this anymore, Angie." He touched the blade to her chunky face.

"Yes you can. We can do it together." To his surprise, he saw less fear in her eyes than he would have expected. Perhaps, in her mind, she longed for an end, too.

"Who are you kidding? As soon as I put this away, you'll call the police. Just like last time." He looked down at his son, who he had never called by his given name: David Junior.

He found in his heart that he did love the boy. His child's tiny eyes stared up at his father in expectation. Even the baby wanted something more than he could offer. This life, this mess that he had created, had to be rectified. And he had to be the one to do it. Love, Drama and all.

The thick blade cut easily though the skin, and David thought he saw Angie close her eyes as small trickles of blood ran down his wounded throat. To his amazement, the pain was minimal; he felt only hot liquid oozing down his chest.

He looked over at his son, and for the first time that night, the boy was not crying: David was.

4

Eddie Roberts didn't live in a penthouse suite, though with the money he sometimes made with the drugs he sold, he often thought he could. He didn't spend a lot of money on frivolous things. In fact, except for his car—a gold-trim Mercedes—he didn't buy any of the other things that his competitors often did. He didn't like bringing attention to himself.

He wasn't stupid. He put that money away. Not in a bank, though. He didn't trust banks. Besides, as soon as they caught onto him, they would seize all his possessions. He had seen that on TV often enough to know better.

And he was sure that they would do it, too. He wasn't at all sure who "they" were, but he knew he despised them. The way he hated cops, cottage cheese, and that old bitch.

Lady Black.

Especially since she kept running around telling everyone about that dope-head son of hers. He didn't care if she was supposed to practice voodoo. He didn't even care if she put one of those spells of hers on him. He just wanted her gone. Just like her son, Jacob.

Torch had run into her a few days before on the corner. She

had been shopping at Sam's market; the package of food hung heavy on the old woman's shoulder. She looked old and worn. He had no doubt that he had done that to her. He smiled at the thought. *Bitch!* How could a woman who could barely carry her own groceries be strong enough to hurt him? He laughed again, adoring the sound of his own echo ringing throughout the empty apartment hall.

He'd be lying if he said that Lady Black didn't hold some kind of fear over him, though. The same fear she held over the other people in the apartment building. It was her eyes. They spoke to him. They told of...

Unrest.

As if she had spent years soaking up the torment around her. Not much different from what he had done, only she seemed to thrive on it. Feed on it. On him.

In any case, he would have to put her out of misery soon. Put a stop to her big mouth. The same way he had done to her son. But Torch had not killed Jacob because he hadn't liked the boy, or because he'd thought Jacob talked too much. In fact, if you asked him, he would have admitted that he had been fond of the boy.

It had just been business.

Jacob had gotten hooked on his stash. He had begun using the drugs he should have sold. Stealing from Torch. Number one rule in dope-school 101: don't mess with your own stash.

Jacob hadn't been the first employee he'd had put down for stealing from him. And he hadn't been the last. But he was the only one that Torch had regretted.

For that, he had made the boy pay. Dearly.

He had driven Jacob out to the neighborhood park just around the corner. There, he had made the boy beg for his life, on his knees. Then he had broken both knees with a hammer. All ten fingers too.

After that, he'd shot Jacob there among the rodents and small animals, as if he'd held no value. Torch couldn't be soft. And if he had let the boy live, he would have been taken as a pussy. His competitors and junkies would have tried to run all over him.

Not him; not Torch. He wouldn't allow it from anyone, especially a no-good junkie dealer. Then Torch had set the body on fire and watched it burn for as long as he could. No one ever knew he had said a prayer for the poor bastard before he set the blaze.

That had been business.

Pleasure had been the young girl from across the street. Chocolate's sister. Even he had to admit that, if he had a vice, it was women. Virgins.

And she had been a virgin. *Sweet. Pure.*

It was hard to believe that she was that whore Chocolate's sister. Chocolate was just another drugged-up junkie with a pussy who would steal any and every thing that she got her hands on. Including his money and his drugs.

Where was Chocolate, anyway?

He hadn't seen her since that night. He hoped that she had gotten the message. If not, he could pay a visit to the two sisters' home. Take that middle one too this time.

She was fine. Then he would have had all three. Sweet. Actually, now that he thought about it, he hadn't seen either of the sisters lately.

Where were they?

He was sure that they wouldn't go to the cops. Maybe they had tried to run.

No matter, he knew that he would be able to find them. Hell, the middle sister worked at the phone company. He would follow her home from work and could find Chocolate then. Hiding away somewhere with his money. *Bitch!*

He wanted his money, his stuff. And he would get it, one way or another.

Deep in the earth at Chocolate Park, Coco Williams stirred. Opened her rotten eyes. They burned.

All the way across town, the grave of Jacob Balan was empty.

The old woman, Lady Black of apartment 3B, worked her black magic in destructive ways. Destructive to the drug dealer, Torch, and to herself.

She kneeled in front of her altar and performed the spells that would bring back to life those who had been long dead. Dead, in some way or another, by the hands of the dealer. And she called upon spirits that she would have to pay tenfold. A price more than she had. She did not care, however; the reward would finally be more than the payment. She would see to that.

In the small pantry-closet, she gripped the blade tightly and repeated her chant for the third time. The blaze of the long red candles flickered, dimmed, but did not extinguish.

She smiled. That meant the gods looked favorably on her offering.

She took this opportunity to give her gift. She cut deeply into the palms of each hand and winced at the pain. The dark droplets fell into the bowl and sizzled as if frying away her sins.

"All that I owe, I pay now."

She laughed, knowing her price, but willing to pay as long as all her debts were repaid, would be received.

One couldn't tell Eddie Roberts that selling drugs was wrong and potentially destructive. Or that burning those who owed him for those drugs, with a lit cigarette, was inhumane. He would have none of it.

His argument—that those who he dealt with were already at the bottom of the human trash-heap, had usually surpassed help, and were destructive to only themselves—always made sense, if to no one but himself.

When he was inside his apartment, alone, without anyone to help, was when they came.

He didn't see them at first, only smelled their presence.

A foul, putrid odor. It smelled of death.

He had only one thought: Lady Black.

He twirled around and saw them. He recognized Coco instantly. Her body had begun to rot, and her dark skin was even darker, but it was her, just the same. She still wore her working clothes: a dull white mini with tassels. Her hair was matted wild in tangles. There were two gunshot holes to her body, and her dress was stained with blood and dirt. Her eyes fixed on him in a stare that hate could not have controlled.

But he had not killed Chocolate, and he had no idea who had. Maybe one of her johns. He was frozen with fear, but his pride refused to let him show it.

He also recognized the dead man with her. Not because of anything that he wore or his eyes—he had none. He simply recognized Jacob because of the pure irony of the situation. The junkies back for the dealer who dealt them a rotten hand.

He almost laughed.

Almost.

Chocolate reached for him and he retreated, more from nausea than from fear. She did not touch him, however, only waved her rotten hand in front of his face, as her spoiled stink consumed his nose.

She stared. Her eyes glowed like a small flame, smaller, then larger, like a wildfire. He couldn't move; she paralyzed him. He began to sweat and realized that the heat was from her hateful gaze.

The flesh on his exposed arms began to flake as small, reddened burn marks appeared. Almost like...cigarette burns. The burns grew hotter and larger, and his entire body felt as if it was on fire from an inner blaze.

He coughed as smoke filled his lungs and shot out of his mouth like that of a car's tailpipe. He was burning from the inside out.

The corpse of Jacob smiled a toothless, lipless grin. Evil. He was enjoying this, just as Eddie would have if he weren't on the receiving end. Dead Jacob touched his shoulder.

Instantly, his arm heated and burst into flame, the ash of his flesh falling to the floor. He screamed and fell to his knees.

Burning flesh—ironic.

He felt no urge to smile this time, as the flames had reached his mouth and he had no lips. He tried to drop to the floor and roll. *Stop. Drop. Roll. Stop. Drop...*

It was no use. An internal flame could not be so easily extinguished.

Dead Jacob and Dead Chocolate watched him burn for as long as they could.

And Eddie "Torch" Roberts had one thought before he was extinguished forever:

Bitch!

Downstairs, in apartment 3B, Lady Black died, her sixty-nine years complete. She had repaid all her debts.

"What She Saw When They Flew Away"

R unning was one of those few freeing experiences in life reserved for the young and the healthy. Unless the young person running wasn't so healthy; then they ran and ran until their little hearts just gave out on them. Pearl knew this to be true. She also knew a lot of things about a lot of things, and at least one thing she just couldn't admit even to herself. She stifled her thoughts, and with her heavy winter coat wrapped tightly around her, she pressed on.

Pearl, not so old in years but looking and feeling as if both her feet were planted firmly in earth soil, made her way home from the bus stop, not making eye contact with anyone or letting anyone make it with her. She passed the Devin twins on the corner and had to suppress the urge to steal one to replace the one she had lost. Not because her baby girl was replaceable, but because she had a hole somewhere in her, and nothing she did seemed to fill it.

The upstairs neighbor stared at her from the ledge, his belly exposed under his open robe, and hanging over his shorts. She didn't acknowledge him. He had never spoken to her, and she had stopped trying to be friendly. At first she had been afraid that he was dangerous, but Mrs. Davis two doors down had said he was harmless, just a bit odd. Still, she didn't like the way he stared at her; there was something about his eyes—most of the time he just stood there watching everyone like a threatening omen over the neighborhood. Sometimes people would go to him if they had questions, but Pearl didn't really know anything about it. She saw people treading in and out of his apartment. If she didn't know better, she'd think he sold drugs. The last time he'd watched her like this, she had gotten the call about her daughter.

Pearl opened the door to her humble apartment on the first floor, letting in a gallon of sunlight, which had been missing in that room for a long time, and flicked the light to the on position and then back off, and then repeated it over again, faster. But the switch didn't work; the room remained dark.

Somewhere in the background she heard scratching noises, but she put them in the back of her head, not knowing what they were, nor really caring. Pearl closed the door behind her, and darkness returned, just as it had for the past three months, six days, and somewhere around four hours. For as long as her daughter had been gone.

Her foot crunched on pieces of broken glass, and from the dim glow through the window she saw a pile of white glass littering the floor. Above her, the light bulb was crushed, and below, a broom lay discarded in the corner.

Someone whispered her name: "Momma."

Just as she thought she was losing her mind completely, she remembered. *She remembered.* She had forgotten her, just for a moment, but longer than any mother should forget a child.

Najya sat slumped on the floor against the wall, holding her right arm. Her eyes were glazed over and she stared off into the distance—to a place that Pearl had not been allowed to go, lately.

"You're bleeding." Pearl didn't like coming home anymore.

The girl looked down absently. "The glass must have cut me when it fell."

Pearl rushed into the bathroom, soaked a towel in water, and came out to wrap it around the girl's arm. Najya jumped a bit from the cold, but let her mother finish. "It doesn't hurt," she said. "I don't feel it."

Everyone had told her that things would be all right soon, and that they would get better with time. Time, they said, healed all wounds, and before she knew it, she and Najya would be happy again. Happy didn't live in that apartment anymore.

The girl looked into her mother's eyes. "They got out again. They're in the walls. Can you hear 'em?" That was what the noise had been; the birds had gotten out. "Why can't they just stay in their cage? I feed them and make sure they have everything they need. What do they want from me?"

Pearl had an idea how they had gotten in there. Before Anaya had died, the girl had put a hole in the wall exactly the size of a big round doorknob. She had been so happy that she had gotten first place in a race that she had thrown the door open without thought, slamming the knob into the plaster, creating the hole. Anaya had been a free spirit, her baby.

Pearl knelt down beside her still-living daughter. "They're birds, baby. They want to be free. You would, too, if you were kept in a cage all the time." The woman looked around her. She wasn't completely sure there was truth to that.

In the summer, they all would go to the beach in Savannah. They didn't have much money, but Pearl always tried to make sure that they spent time with each other. Something cheap or free was always best. She'd take off a few days from work and the three would drive up from Atlanta. She could only afford to be off a few days, and it never seemed like enough time. The motel was always too expensive, and they'd eat cold cuts and sandwiches to defray some of the cost. But she was always proud to be able to provide this small amount of freedom to her children. Sometimes she even managed to feel normal, like the average American who would take her kids on vacation.

The girls loved the water. They'd both stand at the beach's edge while the tide came in, carrying them just a bit farther into the sea. Sometimes the girls would try to do handstands or cartwheels at the water line. She'd watch them, thinking of all the things that could go wrong. There was something about the way the waves washed up, threatening to take them away, that always scared Pearl. She knew at any moment something could happen and take one or both of them away from her. Pearl couldn't swim well. She had never learned. There weren't any swimming pools in Hollywood Court projects, where she had grown up. There had been no community center, nowhere to play or enjoy oneself. The poor didn't swim.

Pearl wanted her daughters to experience things she hadn't as a child. So she pretended to have as much fun as the girls while keeping one eye on each girl at all times—even when they thought she wasn't looking. Even when things unseen terrified her.

At night you could hear them the worst. The birds chirped and scratched at the walls encaging them, perhaps wishing they were back safely in the home Najya kept for them, or perhaps just relishing the freedom they were afforded by being out; Pearl didn't know which. She lay there, staring at the ceiling, listening to Him and Her. Those were their names. Anaya had named them well before she had taken that long run into nowhere. They had bought Her without realizing that she was pregnant, and up until that point they had simply called her "Bird." Now Bird and her son chirped away at the insides of the walls and somewhere at edges of Pearl's sane mind.

She lay there for over an hour, just long enough that she thought for sure that Najya would be asleep—Lord forgive her, she didn't want to see the girl again that night—and made her way to the kitchen.

She didn't make it. Najya had dragged her mattress into the living room and made herself a pad on the floor. The girl stared at her for a long time without saying a word. Her dark skin almost looked purple, dead. She looked like the ghost of her twin sister, Anaya.

Finally, she spoke. "I can hear them better out here. It's so... quiet in my room." Najya and Anaya had shared a room all their lives. She closed her eyes. "I can't remember what she looks like, Momma. I tried, but I just can't."

Pearl lay down beside her daughter and wrapped the twelve-year-old in her arms. She was surprised how well the girl still fit. "Maybe we should put up pictures, ya know? Lots of pictures everywhere. That'll help us remember." Pearl couldn't forget her daughter's face. She had a constant reminder of what Anaya had looked like: Najya.

The girl in her arms broke down. Najya didn't cry very often. In fact, Pearl wasn't sure she had seen her cry at all. She had been too lost in her own emotions, she guessed. "Why did she have to be the one to die? I'm the oldest."

Pearl didn't know what to say, so she didn't say anything at all.

"I feel like half of me's dead. I just don't know what to do. I should have died with her."

"I feel like half of me's dead too."

Najya had covered all of the windows with blankets by the time Pearl got home the next night. The apartment was completely dark. Najya was totally shutting herself off from the rest of the world, Pearl realized.

The girl worked her way into the walls with the biggest knife from the kitchen and a large serving spoon. Bits and pieces of the wall lay discarded on the floor around her, and her kinky black hair was covered in white dust. Her eyes were wide and wild, and she didn't even bother looking at her mother when Pearl called her name. Pearl stood there and watched the girl for a long time. She didn't know what to say. How could she ease the girl's pain when she couldn't even ease her own? What do you say to one child when the other is dead? Everything would certainly *not* be all right like everyone had told them. Things would *not* get better with time.

Najya finally spoke, not taking her eyes off of her work, "They can't leave me too. Do you hear? I won't let them. I need them. How can they run away from me? How can they just fly away?"

Pearl stood there for a moment, and then walked into the kitchen. She grabbed the second-biggest knife from the cabinet and returned to her daughter. She stood over the girl while Najya carved out a large section from the wall, debris thrown everywhere. She didn't know what to do. The girl was in so much pain; she was so lost.

Slowly, Pearl got down on her knees in front of Najya and placed her hands on the girl's shoulders. Najya was tired and panting out of breath, but still she worked to free her birds. Pearl wondered if the girl realized that getting them out was, in effect, caging them, and not the other way around. Najya was hurting, but she was not dumb; she knew.

Pearl held the knife over her head and came down hard. To her surprise, the plaster fell away easily, plummeting to the floor. She worked on her knees beside her daughter for over half an hour. Inside, Him and Her chirped to the rhythm of the knife falls; even they seemed excited. She and Najya were getting closer to the girl's beloved birds—she could feel it.

Beside her, Najya stopped and looked at Pearl as if noticing her for the first time. She seemed so tired, so tired from things greater than freeing a bird from a wall, her mother knew. After a moment, she smiled at Pearl and fell down on the floor, her dark body covered in plaster, content to let her mother help her for a while.

Pearl's blade sank into the wall, and both of them stopped for a moment, not quite sure what they should do now that they had reached their goal. The woman scraped out the remaining hole, careful not to hit one of the birds. Him and Her tweeted louder, their chirps mixing with the pounding of Pearl's heart. She didn't know why, but she was anxious; she had missed the birds, too. She wanted to see them. They represented her dead daughter to her—to them both. She realized this now. They were her Anaya.

Suddenly, Her flew out, golden wings spreading wide as she exited the hole. Just behind her, as he always was, Him flew out, blue and vivid as the light of day. The two circled the room above Pearl and Najya's heads, and then headed toward the patio doors. Najya hadn't covered them; they had probably been too tall for her to reach.

Pearl looked at Najya, slumped beside her. The girl's eyes were wide, wet. "Let them go," she whispered.

"But..."

"Momma, please. Let them go."

Pearl stood—not as fast as she would have liked—and ran through the kitchen. She unlocked the glass doors and threw them open. The birds hesitated before the mother led her son out of the house and into the world.

They flew wild and free, as she had never seen them before, and after a while, they were completely out of sight. She watched for a while longer, and then closed the doors behind them.

"He Who Takes the Pain Away"

Get back in that bed, girl. You go on to sleep," Mama said, clinging tightly to her apron. Hattie Mae let the curtain fall back into place and ran to bed with her tiny ebony feet patting on the hardwood floor as she went. She scooted in next to her sister, Betsy, and snuggled under the tattered covers, awaiting Mama's kiss.

And of course Mama didn't fail her. Her lips were soft and moist despite the worn, tired look on her face. She sighed as she stood back up, holding her back. Evidence of a long, hard life, Mama always said.

"Now you go on to sleep, girl."

The girl nodded and closed her eyes. She heard Mama cut off the lights and pull the door shut. It squeaked just before it closed all the way. Mama hadn't pulled the door completely shut, Hattie Mae knew it would have been too dark. Hattie Mae didn't like the dark.

When she opened her eyes, the room was almost completely black, except for the light from the hall and that of the street post outside her window. She could hardly see past her own nose.

Neither of the lights reached as far as her bed.

The shadows on the walls shifted and changed in the strange way that they sometimes did at night, and she stared, hoping to see Him somewhere within them.

"What are you doin'?" Betsy whispered, holding her hand over her mouth as she coughed. "Mama's gonna skin you if she finds you awake again."

"I thought you were 'sleep. She'll skin you too."

"Un um." She shook her wobbly head. "I'm smart enough to pretend sleep. You ain't." Betsy elbowed her in the side. It didn't hurt, though; she wasn't that strong anymore.

The wall pictures shimmered again, and this time Hattie Mae thought she saw the outline of a man within them. "I think I just saw him," she said with a smile.

She pulled the covers back and started to get out of bed, but her sister grabbed her arm and held her in place. "He'll put pepper in your eyes. Now get to sleep."

Hattie Mae heard Mama cleaning and washing the dishes from supper. She had just turned off the water when there was a loud thumping sound from the roof.

"He's here," Hattie Mae said with all the excitement that only an eight-year-old can have. She bounced up and down on the bed, making the springs squeak and moan under the strain.

Just then she heard Mama's footfalls coming toward their room. Betsy must have heard them too.

"Told you." Then she put her head back down, pretending to sleep.

Mama burst into the room, not bothering to turn on the lights as she made her way over to the bed. "Thought I said to get to sleep, Hattie Mae. He's comin'. Heard 'im on the roof just now. You better get on to sleep, 'for he put pepper in your eyes." She put her hands on her large hips. "Now don't make me swat you, girl."

Betsy sat up, wiping her eyes and pretending to wake up. "What's wrong, Mama?"

But Mama knew better, "Don't play with me, girl. If you were really sleep, you would've woke up with all that bouncin' up and down. I heard it all the way in the kitchen."

There was another loud thump from the rooftop, and Mama almost jumped out of her skin. When she looked back down at the girls, Hattie Mae thought she saw fear in the old woman's eyes. Mama smiled and bent down to kiss them both on the forehead. Hattie Mae reached out to hug her mama. "Is He here, Mama?" She whispered into her ear.

This time she was *sure* that she saw tears in her mama's eyes; the woman, who had grown old beyond her years, wiped them away fast.

"I think He is, baby."

Hattie Mae smiled at Betsy. "Black Man's here." Then she looked to her mama and asked, "Will he take it away, Mama?"

"Yes, baby. He'll take it all away. Did you kiss your sister good night?"

Hattie Mae nodded her head.

Suddenly, a shadow loomed behind Mama, completely engulfing her dark skin into the blackness, making her a shadow within a shadow. The room became colder, and Hattie Mae could see her breath as she spoke. "He's here."

The shadow seemed to shrink into itself and form the outline of a man. A very tall, dark, featureless man. For the life of her, she could swear that he didn't have a face. The shadow man glided toward Mama. He moved with an unnatural agility and seemed to float on nothing but the air itself, and for the first time, Hattie Mae thought that she should be afraid of him.

The man began to speak, his voice a soft whisper. "I'm here for your sick."

Mama moved aside slowly to let the shadow man by. She seemed to have a mixed look on her face: half-mournful, half proud. As if she thought that just by doing this she had blessed them and cursed them all at the same time. Hattie Mae knew from experience that was just what her mama thought, for the shadow man had taken her father, too.

The man reached her bed in just two steps, whereas it would have taken her more than ten, and slowly bent over and touched Betsy's head.

His fingers sank right into her skin as a sharp bright light was expelled from the wound.

Hattie Mae couldn't see the light through the cover of her own eyelids, however. She didn't want to see what would happen. When she opened them, the shadow man was gone. "Did He take it, Mama?"

"He took it, baby."

Hattie Mae sat up in her bed, afraid to look over at the spot where her sister should have been—*had* been for her entire life. She slowly turned her head.

Betsy was gone.

Mama said, "God bless He Who Takes Away the Pain."

The lady nurse came the next day. She stood at the door with her sharp white pants and white blouse (*You can't trust a woman in pants*, Mama always said) and her big black bag.

"Ain't no sick here," Mama said as soon as she opened the door.

"I would be willing to just check out your girl there." She winked at Hattie Mae. "What could it hurt?"

Mama shook her head. "She ain't sick. Don't need no doctor here."

"Oh," the woman shot a big smile, "I'm not a doctor. I'm just someone who wants to ease the suffering. That's all."

"We got Him for that."

"I'm sure you do. But—" she smiled again "—what can it hurt? Just some time and a little bit of hope. It won't cost you a thing."

"Look," Mama said, "we don't need no healers here. Gettin 'em riled up. Makin 'em think that God ain't meant for them to suffer. Tryin' to turn them away from Him."

The woman shook her tiny head. "I just want to help ease the pain a little. That's all. Maybe save a life or two along the way."

"We was put here to die. Now get. Ain't no sick here." Mama slammed the door.

When she spun around she caught Hattie Mae staring at her. "Hattie Mae, you get in there and do them chores. And empty that trash, girl."

Outside, Hattie Mae pulled the can behind her like it weighed a ton—and it did, to her. *Betsy used to do this, before she was gone,* she thought. *Now I gotta do it. I hate doin' the trash.* Just as she picked up the heavy can and tried to lift it into the bend, the weight lightened and it was lifted right out of her arms.

She looked up to see the nurse's pearly white teeth smiling at her, her dark skin a strange contrast to those bright whites.

"Hi."

"Hey." Hattie Mae looked around. She knew she wasn't supposed to be talking to this woman, but she had to admit that she liked her.

They had lived in a place called Baltimore before they'd come here, and Hattie Mae knew that not everybody lived like this. She just wanted everything to be like it was before. She just wanted hope. But there was no hope; Papa and Betsy were gone.

"So, what's your name?"

"Hattie Mae," she whispered.

"Oh, that's a pretty name. Boy, I wish I had a pretty name like that."

"What is your name?"

She smiled. "I have no name for which they call me outright. Not to my face, anyway." She laughed, and her entire face lit up like the wick of a newly ignited candle. "But you may name me if you like."

"Well, I don't know. Ain't never named nobody b'fore. Papa said that pickin' names for us girls was the hardest thing he ever had to do. Ends up he just named me after his Mama and Betsy after Mama's mama." Hattie Mae looked at the ground as if she had said something wrong.

The woman smiled. "Go on, you can do it."

"Well, how 'bout Joy? Always liked that name."

The woman thought about it for a moment. "I like that. Joy." She let the word linger on her tongue for a moment. "Joy."

"Maybe Mary, like the mother of Christ. Or Sarah. That's in the Bible too."

"I like them all."

"I really like Mary," Hattie Mae said, just as her Mama opened the back door to their small shotgun house, calling her name.

"Well, then…" the woman bent over so that the two were eye to twinkling eye, "…why don't you get back to me on it? Okay?" She winked.

When the girl watched her walk away, it almost looked as if she were walking straight into the sun itself. Hattie Mae got a warm feeling all over her body.

"Let he who knows pain and fear, know Him. Those with doubt in their hearts and hate on their minds will not see Him."

The preacher's voice boomed through the small church room. Everyone sat motionless and quiet. Every once in a while a loud "Amen!" would ring out from the onlookers, but it did not interrupt the showman's flow.

"And do not be fooled by those she-devils with the short skirts and long legs. For they are the work of evilness. Man was placed here and woman came next to tempt him. But do not be tempted." He screamed his warning, pointing his bony finger into the crowd. "She will *damn* you." He paused and looked around, eyeing each and every one in the humble room. To Hattie Mae, it seemed as if he held her gaze for an eternity.

"But He who takes your pain will come. And He will save you. All you must do is ask. Like a child on Christmas, you'll be happy. Sickness comes and there will be those who tell you to run to those doctors. Those she-devils. Those unholy folk who don't give a damn about your soul; they only want your body. But that's sinful. If God wants you well, he'll heal you."

"Amen!" Someone shouted.

"That's sinful. Sinful." He ended his sermon, repeating that word with particular heinousness. "Sinful."

The church members were spellbound, as they usually were when the man spoke. Most stayed late to help him with some odd chore or another and to applaud the minister on his insightful revelation.

Pastor Zackaria was said to have the gift of sight, as was his father before him. And his father before that.

Hattie Mae and her mama walked over, and her mother shook the man's hand. He held it tightly, cupping it with the other. "He came to us last night, Father."

"Praise the Lord," the preacher said. "She's walking with the angels now, sister."

Hattie Mae's Mama nodded her head. "And with her father."

The days and months passed. Every now and again the woman without a name would come to visit, and Mama would slam the door in her face. The outside world moved along as it always did, while the members stuck together on the tiny island began dying.

Hattie Mae saw the woman nurse going to other people's houses, but they all shunned her, just as Mama had. The girl began to overhear the adults whisper about "smallpox." She didn't know why, but that word scared her. They said that some of the deliverymen had brought it over on the boat from Africa when they delivered supplies.

A pregnant cloud of hopelessness hung over the group. Night after night, He Who Takes Away the Pain also took the members' loved ones. One night it was Mr. Carson, the next it was Mrs. Black and her unborn child.

The schoolhouse was virtually empty, as only Hattie Mae and three other children were well enough to come. And then it closed altogether when the teacher, Mrs. Carson, went away with Him.

That night, Hattie Mae awoke to find Him standing over her bed, His icy hand on her forehead.

She felt the sickness run through her body as He caressed her face. She felt the deadly presence of something older than time touching her soul. And she knew that she, like her father and sister, would be taken away soon.

The next day in church, there were very few people. Most of the five hundred or so people who had originally come here with Pastor Zackaria had either gone or were too sick to attend. Hattie Mae knew that they, like her family, would never get better. Her mama had died during the night, and He had come to claim her.

Hattie Mae tried not to mourn her—like Mama had instructed her before she'd died—but she cried like a little baby alone in that house. She hated to be alone.

Pastor Zackaria also showed signs of the sickness as he sat and spoke, telling everyone not to be afraid, that the end would come soon enough. But the "Amens" had been replaced by the coughs and moans of the sick.

Just then, the doors to the church burst open, leaving the splintered wood to hang freely from the hinges, and the lady nurse without a name walked in. She didn't carry her big black bag since no one there could be helped anymore.

She walked—almost glided—to the front of the church and stood at the altar. Although her lips did not move, the group could hear her voice clearly in their heads.

"The last of you has been infected now. You were offered the opportunity to help yourselves. To save yourselves and your children from the suffering of death and pain. But you refused." Still, her mouth did not move, and her eyes blinked wildly. "He who takes away your pain—your children's pain—also takes away their lives. But—" she paused and held out her hands "—she who stands before you now could have taken away your sorrow as well."

And with that, she was gone. Her beautiful, magnificent light faded into a dull glow, and then into a pin-sized light, and then disappeared altogether.

The group of fewer than ten people sat in silence for a complete minute, stunned, unable to speak.

Then, the pastor's voice erupted, a hollow shell of what it had once been. "I ask you all now, what is pain without suffering?"

Everyone applauded in agreement, the horrendous coughs echoing throughout the dead room.

Hattie Mae looked up to the sky, hoping somehow to see the unnamed nurse. She dared to name her: Hope.

"CUE: CHANGE"

CUE: Me running for my life. The zombies didn't really chase you, as much as they loomed menacingly. There was something in their demeanor that signaled they were the zombies—that they were changed and not like the rest of us. Of course, I had heard the rumors about the inner cities and that people were looting and rioting in the streets. But hell, they were *my* streets. And I never believed white folks until I saw evidence for myself. Call it a survival mechanism.

Survival was what had me running for my life at that moment. I had been out hustling when I realized that perhaps zombies did exist. Now, hustling may seem like a questionable occupation, but really it just meant that I was working. At Walmart, no less. I was a sales associate, which was a fancy term for cashier. It wasn't a Walmart in my own neighborhood—there weren't any there. I was in some ritzy part of town where people actually spent good money on Kleenex to wipe their noses instead of using plain toilet paper like the rest of us.

I was waiting on some chick with too much money to spend on dyeing her hair a color that no human being had ever been born with, and suddenly she reach out to touch me. You have to understand the dynamic in this situation before you realize that this was odd. These people didn't touch me; most of them placed their money on the roller to keep from touching me. And they didn't care if their money or sometimes their credit cards rolled right down the hatch, they'd just take out more.

So when this woman reached for me, I recoiled out of reflex. Then she leaned in and whispered, "It doesn't hurt. I just need to touch you, to taste you." Her eyes rolled toward the back of her head for a moment while she sniffed the air, evidently *smelling* me.

I looked at the woman, and then around the store. Almost everyone there was staring back at me. Over in the corner near the door, a very large white man dropped to the floor and several people crowded in, attacking him. I stared at them long enough to know that I should probably get my black ass out of there. I picked up the biggest weapon I could find—an extra long, extra hard salami roll—and backed slowly toward the door. Then I ran my black ass right back to the one part of world where I knew I'd be safe. The projects.

CUE: How all this went down. When one homeless man eats another on the streets of Chicago, it's unfortunate; if he eats a businessman on his way home from the office, it's a tragedy; and when it happens on the six o'clock news, it's a national emergency.

It started in the inner cities. Large, dark gangs of the homeless and street people began looting and attacking. The media dubbed it "crime sprees typical of the demographic"—as if random homeless people across the nation had the means or funding to revolt on their own. They urged everyone not to panic, of course, while showing brutal scenes of people rioting in the streets, which caused the natural reaction of...panic.

Inside the cities there was chaos. No one knew how to contain them, at first thinking they were simply out of control—marching for some form of civil rights that they had long since gotten. Then, more and more began to join their ranks. It was rumored that people were dying in the streets by the hundreds. Finally, the news called them an "unstable horde," which sought to undermine the very idea of our society.

CUE: The mass flooding of news media into the cities—to become lunch. Actually, if anyone knew anything about the media, they'd realize that no one could have a filling meal from the bastards; at best, they could be a light snack. But everyone outside of the cities watched on in horror and astonishment, tucked safely within the comfort of their suburban homes.

At that point, the police and military were sent out to stabilize the massive crowds, and everyone across the country finally began to feel safe again. Soon the police and military were fighting *with* the hordes. Television depicted images of uniformed officers attacking other uniformed officers. The cops were armed with batons and guns but didn't bother to use them as they stormed through the barricades followed by the homeless. And they were *eating* each other. As the camera zoomed in, the entire country saw—in an endless loop that played day and night—a large cop grab another and tear a small, almost superficial, gash into his cheek. It was in L.A. this time. The bitten man stumbled backward as several others swarmed in, crowding him. Finally, he was completely out of the camera shot and presumed dead.

Soon, we realized that the dead didn't stay dead. Like zombies.

CUE: All the experts on national talk shows discussing the walking dead. The implausibility of the idea. Or the real-life incident that was supposed to have happened somewhere that no one could agree on. Whatever. It didn't matter. If there was a scientist or "expert" to be found, they were put on TV.

By this time it didn't really matter what the experts had to say because people outside the city were being attacked too. The hordes abandoned the cities en masse in the same way that everyone with any means to do so left it eventually. Only, the zombies didn't care about property values. They didn't really seem to care about anything except hunting people down and killing them.

There were rumors that a bullet to the head would not kill them. It was hard to say, at first, because anyone who ever got close enough to them didn't really live to tell about it. But it was clear that these zombies weren't quite your average drop dead, get up, roam the countryside eating brains zombies. And they weren't drugged out on puffer fish juice either. They...talked. Which meant they were smart. They were said to have some kind of social agenda—they spoke of evolution and social change. No one listened.

One by one entire, cities began to overhaul themselves—though I wasn't sure what overhaul meant. It eventually became clear that the zombies weren't looting in the cities as had previously been reported; they were *infecting* the cities, one person at a time. They weren't stealing, they were *changing*. No one likes change. It scares people.

All these things the experts discussed over and over again while the average people locked away in their homes were eaten into zombies. Until the day the electricity stopped working.

CUE: Me. The idiot who tried to go to work at Walmart during this madness, and who now had to figure out how to get the electricity back on, or at least find a working, not-currently-in-use generator to keep twenty adults and twice as many children able to see how to take a piss without threatening to burn the building down with candles. But the lights weren't the only problem; it was the electricity in general. You see, Carl's grandmother used a ventilator to breathe. Carl was twelve years old and sat by the woman's side night and day. Now he and a few others watched for signs of distress and used a hand-held breathing pump to keep her alive. This couldn't go on for much longer.

The problem, as I saw it, was that if the zombies were as smart as everyone said they were, they had probably cut the electricity, and if they were *really* smart, they already knew we were there. Thus, leaving would in essence be opening ourselves up for trouble. But I dealt in odds—whatever was the best option at the moment. I'm a kid of the streets; I was born here, and I was sure I'd die here. I was okay with that. At that moment, my best option was to at least try to get the electricity back on. The bad part was that I had to do it during a zombie attack.

"You sure about this, kid?"

Japa was old and had earned the right to call anyone kid. But he called me that because that was what everyone called me. Always had. Japa had lived in this building for as long as I could remember. We all had. He was a city man, a long-time resident of the streets, he said, but a short-time visitor of life. He fancied himself a poet; everyone else considered him a wise man. His white hair of wool sat nearly five inches high on his head, and when he stared at you, his eyes seemed darker than his black skin.

"Not really." I didn't really look into Japa's eyes. He was much taller than me. "But supplies are low, and even with the candles we got, it'll be completely dark within a week. And we have to try to do something for Carl—he'll lose it if she dies. You know that."

Japa stared at me, but I ignored him and continued loading my backpack. I didn't expect to be gone long, but just in case something went wrong, I needed to have provisions. I hadn't left the building since that day. None of us had. There were advantages to living in the housing projects when something like this went down.

CUE: *Hollywood Hills* housing development in southwest Atlanta, Georgia. A run-down place that's supposed to conjure images of beautiful, comfortable flats with happy families that are meant to make the uptown folks feel happy about where they spent money, and even happier that they didn't have to stay there themselves. The

Hills was a place where people cared about each other, took food to the sick, and defended themselves against outside threats, whatever those might be. Right then, those threats were the walking dead. Prior to that they had been the police officers who attacked whoever they thought looked "suspicious;" a white man in a big black Cadillac who roamed the neighborhood and got too handsy with the little girls; or anyone who thought that the people in Hollywood Hills were weak and vulnerable because of our lack of money.

We didn't have money, but we refused to be victims. The police regularly got rocks thrown at them, or, as terrible as the thought is, they got shot at after particularly brutal beatings of the men of the complex. The Cadillac man was dragged from his car and beaten by the corner dealers. He refused to press charges. Others were handled as needed. People had a right to protect their homes. That didn't change just because you lived in a poor neighborhood.

In fact, some may say that our special garden variety of zombie was actually less threatening than the brutal police or rich perverts who had roamed our streets previously. At least they weren't licensed by corrupt laws. That was how I saw it. It was how a lot of people saw it.

After the news warned us to stay in the house, each separate building in the Hollywood Hills complex took caution however they saw fit. Our building barricaded the doors. There were only two ways out of the building. In the beginning, it had been meant to ensure that people were effectively caged like animals, but after the zombie attack, it ensured that we only had two doors to guard. Of course, that also meant there were only two ways to escape. But you had to take what you had—and we had children to protect. Then we pulled together and rationed the food and necessary items (at the end of the world, certain things become more valuable than others: batteries, flashlights, meds, etc.). We put three armed guards who worked in shifts on each door. The building was run like an old-fashioned boarding school: everyone ate, everyone had a job.

The end of the world had happened three weeks earlier. We weren't really sure what had happened since then, only heard the vague TV or radio reports. Although we were pretty well stocked on food—shit, that's what food stamps were for—now that the electricity was off, the food would go bad if we didn't find a way to stop it.

We radioed each of the other buildings by walkie-talkie and

told them our plans. Each building agreed and sent one person out with me. There were a total of five of us: me; Allen, an unemployed electrician from building two; Simms, a dealer from number one; Slow Walker, a user from five; and from building four, there was Tiny, a giant man who no one really knew anything about.

I exited my building after scoping as best as I could through the twelve-by-twenty inch window. The guards opened the door quickly and scanned the area, guns drawn, and I stepped out into the new world. The air smelled fresh—not like inside. It was quiet. Too quiet. Nothing moved or sang or chirped or breathed. Not even me. As soon as I took a step, the sound of my foot crunching on leaves was the loudest sound I had heard in weeks. I stopped and looked around. Still nothing stirred. Then I ran to number five as fast as I dared.

We had all agreed on the walkie that we'd meet there, since it was closer to the street and still hidden from view of onlookers, or in this case the walking dead. They must have seen me coming because they opened the door, and I slid inside just before it closed.

"What's up, Kid?" Slow Walker slapped my palm and hit me with the customary one arm hug. The man was tall, mostly legs, and took long, deliberate strides when he walked.

"Same shit, different day." I looked around. Someone was missing. "Where's Allen?"

Simms nodded toward deeper into the building. "Taking a piss. Nerves."

The halls were almost completely dark, and we all waited for the man in silence. In shadow, Tiny looked bigger than he ever had in the daylight. Slow Walker was almost his height, but had nowhere near his bulk. Simms was probably the baddest person in that room—carried a gun whether there were zombies roaming around outside or not—but only stood about five feet tall. She called herself a bitch, but dared anyone else to.

Allen came down the hall with a flashlight, zipping his fly, the light bouncing up and down across the walls. I'd known him about a year, since he and his family had moved to Hollywood Hills. His wife was close to my mother. He nodded when he saw me.

The main discussion was over whether to drive or take a car. Slow Walker insisted that he'd heard vehicles driving past steadily over the last few weeks, as if nothing had changed. We didn't really believe him, though. The man was high half the time, and the other half he was trying to get high. Either way, we'd be harder to catch by slow-moving zombies in a car, and easier to be seen by other survivors. So it was decided. Simms had a Navigator that she'd brought from the auction for eight grand. We took that.

The roads were empty. Nothing human moved. A dog ran across the road in front of the SUV, stopped, looked at us as if it'd never seen a person before. It wasn't too confused by the power dynamic, however, because as we got closer it ran away to keep from getting run over. But other than that, except for the old news media images that we'd all seen, and the woman at Walmart trying to hold my hand, I would swear that nothing at all had happened. Where was everyone, we wondered.

We tried the radio in the car, but none of the stations worked anymore. It was for the best. We were scared and any little news would have just made it worse. In the back seat, Slow Walker sat between Allen and Tiny. The man's long, bony fingers twitched, as if aching to touch something. He watched them, looking up every now and again to see if anyone noticed. I watched from my passenger-side visor's mirror. Then Allen reached out and touched the tall man's hand, wrapping his fingers around both of Slow Walker's hands to slow the trembles. It was such a deliberate show of affection, I almost smiled. Everyone knew Slow Walker was a junkie. Most people avoided him. As did I.

Just as I felt as if I was intruding on this personal matter, Slow Walker lifted his eyes to mine and stared at me through the mirror. Junkies didn't like to be stared at. I had forgotten obvious social graces while stuck in that building for those weeks. I closed the visor and decided to mind my own damn business.

CUE: The Southwest Utility complex, which was only about a mile and a half away from The Hills. We figured that from there Allen could get in and work out how to get things turned back on. He assured us that he knew hardly anything about the utility company's main supply, but we thought it wouldn't hurt to try. Allen agreed that he would do what he could when he got there.

We ran into the first horde there. They stood around the gate, staring at something inside. There were hundreds of them, just standing around. Simms pulled the car off to the side, hidden from view. I pulled out a pair of binoculars (another one of those necessary items in an apocalypse) and watched. They moved slowly, deliberately. I began to wonder if they were really zombies at all. There weren't any missing limbs, and there were no abnormal bloody, torn gashes in anyone. Some held hands and swayed counterclockwise in a circle, as if they were meditating or something. I handed the binoculars over to Simms. She let out a soft gasp.

"What is it?" Tiny asked. She handed the binoculars to the back seat. Each took a turn watching the group of seemingly normal people. "What are they doing?"

"My guess is ensuring that people like us don't get in. The damnedest thing, though. They look so...normal. Why do they look so normal?" Simms was asking a rhetorical question, and it wasn't like we actually knew the answer, so no one responded.

"I said why the fuck do they look so normal, Goddamn it!" Man, I had misjudged that one.

"I was thinking the same thing," I said, just to respond. Then I started thinking about it. "What if that's the plan, really. They're supposed to be smart, right? Well, what if they're smart enough to disguise themselves as normal people? Then all they have to do is wait."

"Wait. Wait for what?" Allen asked; his voice was trembling.

"Us."

Suddenly, someone screamed. Loudly. The group parted as two people were dragged through the crowd and placed on the ground. Placed—not thrown, I noted. The zombies moved back and forth, fidgeting, their hands opening and closing, as if they were anxious. But something was keeping them from attacking. The two women—I could see that now—hugged each other.

"Shit shit shit shit shit," Simms kept repeating behind me. "We can't just sit here. Damn it to hell. We can't." Before anyone could stop her, she jumped out of the car and crouched behind the bushes and drew her gun.

"Shit." I jumped out behind her and motioned for the others to stay in the car. I would get Simms and bring her back. If I couldn't, I'd dash back and drive away. Between the five of us we had seven guns, and that was only because Simms had three. We couldn't afford to lose her. But even so, we couldn't help those women and we could die trying. When I reached the bushes, I bent down beside her and whispered, "What the hell are you doing?"

She ignored me and watched the dead play with their food.

One of the women stood up and pulled out a gun. She helped the other woman to her feet. But the second woman was wobbly and her leg looked broken. She leaned on the first, who held the horde off by gunpoint.

"I swear to God, I'll shoot." The woman was screaming for no reason; even I heard her from my position. The gun quivered in her hand, pointing back and forth at the dead people in the crowd. The group didn't make a move for the women as they backed away. They couldn't get far, though; there were a lot of zombies and only two of them. Finally, one of the horde broke away and moved toward the women, its hand outstretched. The thing seemed to be reasoning with her. *Reasoning?*

Simms turned to look at me. The woman fired; the shot went through the zombie's head. The impact threw the body backward, its hands still outstretched as it fell to the ground. Just as the zombie fell, the woman with the broken leg lost her balance and fell to the ground. The dead simply looked on as another walked forward to take the fallen zombie's place, and it, too, was shot—this time in the chest. It fell too. *So*, I thought, *the reports were wrong. They do die.*

As each zombie died, another moved in to take its place, and it, too, died. Until, of course, the woman ran out of bullets. The gun clicked over and over again before she realized that nothing was coming out. The horde stopped advancing. They just stopped, looked at the women. Then something very strange happened.

A small child walked from within the crowd, placed her tiny hands on the cheek of the woman with the broken leg, and wiped away the woman's tears. The girl began to cry too. Before the woman on the ground could stop herself, she scooped the girl into her arms and hugged her. The child's plaits were held together by large red bows, and the two held onto each other as if they belonged together.

Seeing this, the woman with the gun sank to her knees and burst out crying. She screamed loud and long. Finally, one of the horde, a man with a discernable limp, walked to her and held the woman. Just as she was about to sink into his embrace, something snapped in her. I could see it in her posture; she stiffened and jerked away from him. Suddenly, she reached out and punched the zombie, who recoiled backward. Not in pain, I could tell, but in shock. He actually looked sad that she had rejected him.

I all but forgot about Simms or the others in the car as I watched the woman beat and claw her way through the crowd of undead. She dashed toward us, hiding in the bushes. As soon as she was so close I could smell her sweat and fear, one of the creatures tackled her and brought her to the ground. He spoke softly, soothingly. "Don't fight. You may not survive if you're injured." Still, she fought, kicking and screaming. He grabbed her shoulders. "Don't."

Another man walked over and helped her to her feet. He held the woman's wrist tightly, but as gently as possible. I remember thinking that I shouldn't know these things. But I felt like I had somehow gotten into their heads, or that I could read their body language better than the average human. It was as if they were completely open, like all of their feelings and actions were gliding on the airwaves, infecting everyone around. Beside me, even Simms had calmed down, her .45 automatic hanging limply at her side.

The second man let the woman go and spoke clearly, calmly. "We don't want to have to kill you. There have been too many deaths today. You have taken seven, and there are only two of you to replace those of us who were lost. They sacrificed themselves to protect you. We won't accept any more losses." As he spoke, his hands twitched, and he began to open and close them, as if to keep them busy. "You belong with us, sister." He reached out his hand to her.

She looked around, searching for something, someone to help her. We continued to hide. When no one came to her rescue, she reluctantly grabbed his large, dark fingers. Shaking, he brought her hand to his mouth and bit her, tearing the skin only slightly. The rest walked to her, some scratching, other simply touching her as if to affirm and welcome her into the fold.

After a moment of this interaction, the woman fell to the ground, trembling. Two people from the crowd carried her to her friend, who had also passed out. Someone covered the pair with a thick, colorful blanket. They waited.

"What the hell is going on, Kid?" Simms asked me. "What are these things?"

The horde turned toward us slowly, as if they'd heard her.

They stared through the shrubs that hid Simms and me, directly at us. But none of them moved to attack.

"We better go." We ran to the car and pulled away. Through the passenger side mirror I watched as the horde watched us leave.

"What in the hell just happened?" Tiny asked.

"I don't know. But those things..." I didn't know what to say. "...if those things are zombies, I'll fucking eat my shoe."

In the back seat, Slow Walker was fast asleep. He startled, mumbling something under his breath.

"How long has he been like this?" I asked.

"Pretty much the whole time," Allen said.

"Who in the hell's idea was it to bring him?" Tiny sounded pissed. "He's always like this. It never even matters if he's high or not. He always shakes like he's withdrawing or something. This is stupid." Something told me that Tiny was scared, and this was simply a way for him to vent his frustration, so I didn't say anything to him about Slow Walker. The truth was that I agreed with him. I had no idea why his building chose for him to go with us, considering his history. But now that I thought about it, perhaps I did know. Perhaps they wanted to get rid of him. They had probably simply chosen the most expendable person in the building. What did it matter if he didn't come back? He was all but useless anyway. I had volunteered to go, and Tiny had probably been chosen because of his brute strength, as had Simms. Walker had simply been the last person anyone cared about. It was sad, but that was how things were in this new world of zombies and survival of the fittest.

I thought about the housing projects in which I had lived my entire life and the zombies that I had seen and heard only moments before. Perhaps that was always how things had been, and they were really the ones who were different. Hadn't seven died in order to save just two people? Who was I kidding? They were zombies. They were probably lying to get her to do what they wanted. Well, why not just attack her?

I didn't like where my thoughts were taking me. Zombies were the bad guys—if you could call them guys—and we were the good guys. If you'd asked me at the time who "we" were, I wouldn't have quite known. I had lived twenty years knowing that I was just as expendable as Slow Walker. Like him, the only thing that I had done wrong was be born the wrong...everything. Nothing about me was acceptable within my own country. It was so bad that I was honestly considering the insane option of being a zombie over my own life.

The hardware store was two miles from the utility complex and three and a half miles from The Hills. If we rushed, we could get there, get gas, and get back home before dark and before any of the memories of the day had a chance to etch themselves into our brains. I hoped.

Inside, we each grabbed a shopping cart and headed toward the generators. I wanted to get as much water and other supplies as possible too, because you could never have too much stuff. The store looked deserted. There were no lights, but the big front windows lit up most of the inside of the building. It was amazing, but almost nothing in the store looked touched. It was as if no one had thought of coming here, yet. I was sure that any Walmart or somewhere just as commercial would be bare by this point. Considering the way people behaved in Georgia when there was only a snow alert, imagine the insanity when under the threat of zombie attack.

Just as I turned the corner, a man stood in my way, pointing a pistol at my head. I stopped, didn't say a word. In the background, I could hear the others talking to each other, assuring each person that everything was fine. It wouldn't be too long before they realized they hadn't heard my voice.

"What the hell do you want?" the guy whispered.

I held my hands up in the air, not wanting to piss him off. "Nothing. Just supplies and stuff."

"Just supplies and stuff," the man mocked. "My supplies. My stuff." His blue eyes shone just like they did in all the books I'd read. It looked like the man might be getting ready to cry.

"I'm sorry, man, we didn't mean any harm. We just needed stuff because all the lights just went out—" Before I could finish, Tiny grabbed the man under his arms and put him in a full nelson headlock so he couldn't move. I walked up and took the gun from the man.

"I'm gonna let you go, but I don't want no shit from you or I'll break your kneecaps, you hear?" Tiny could be really threatening when he needed to. Actually, with his body size, he didn't really need to most of the time. Tiny slowly lowered the man to the ground, and for the first, time I realized that he had lifted him off the floor. The others came running to us, having heard Tiny.

"What's going on?" Allen asked.

"Nothing. This fool pulled a gun on me."

"Who are you?" Simms said.

"This was my place before you guys broke in."

"Broke in my ass," she said. "The damn door was opened."

"It was unlocked, not opened." The man was a smartass.

"Fuck you, man," Tiny said. "It don't belong to you no more than it belongs to us."

Simms squinted her eyes, got in the man's face. "Shit, ya'll know who this is? This here's Cadillac Man." Before the man could respond, she reached out and punched him in the jaw. "You like preying on little girls, Cadillac Man?" The man fell to the ground, holding his face.

"Are you sure that's him?" I asked.

She lifted her foot and stomped his leg. "I'm sure." Simms had almost beaten this man to death once. Looked like she relished the opportunity to finish the job.

"Wait a minute." Allen stopped her before she could kick the man again. "You... you don't know this is him."

"The hell I don't. Get your goddamn hands off me." She jerked away from him. "Ask him."

Allen bent down and touched the man, who jumped as if afraid. Simms sighed, not buying any of the man's whiny bullshit.

"Sir, what's your name?" The man looked at Allen, then rolled his eyes. "She'll hurt you and we won't be able to stop her. What's your name?"

"Picket," Simms said. "That was the perv's name."

Still the man did not answer. Tiny walked over and pulled the man's wallet from his back pocket, opened it. "Samuel Picket."

Simms kicked him again. "I told you."

"Don't do that again," Allen warned her.

I looked around. Someone was missing again, and I was getting tired of having to keep count. "Where's Walker?"

"He ran away," Allen said.

"The hell you mean, he ran away?"

"I don't know. I looked up and saw him dash outta of the store. He probably just needed some air."

Simms walked up to Allen and grabbed his T-shirt by the

absent collar. "What the hell, man? We don't leave people, and we don't let sick people wander around alone."

"How was I supposed to stop him?" He grabbed her hand tightly, and she winced in pain.

Before the two could get started yelling at each other again, I said, "You could have told us. We would have got him, brought him back. What are we supposed to do now? Shit." I looked at the man on the floor, then out the window. It would be getting dark soon, and I didn't want to have to leave without Slow Walker. *Why not?*

"Maybe he's headed home already," Tiny said. "You know Slow Walker. He does his own thing."

A loud noise erupted from outside. On the floor, Cadillac Man began laughing.

CUE: The point at which you would actually rather be in hell than deal with what's coming next.

As Cadillac Man lay on the floor laughing, we headed to the front of the building. Outside, a large group of people, more than twice the size of the group we had seen only a few hours before, stood staring at the building. The sun was setting, but it was summertime and only seven o'clock in the evening. We had more than an hour before the sun set completely, plunging the entire block into darkness. It didn't matter, though; we wouldn't last that long.

"Shit shit shit shit shit shit," Simms repeated again. "We can't get past that. Damn it. There're too many of them."

Behind us, Tiny hit the floor hard. He began convulsing and shaking so hard I thought maybe he was having a heart attack. Allen rushed to his side to help him. Cadillac Man continued laughing. Simms reached down and hit the man with the butt of her gun. He screamed in pain and began rocking and moaning while holding his legs to his chest in a tight ball. Simms hit him again. Then again.

Allen walked up and put his hand on her shoulder. "Don't kill him. Please." She kicked him this time, not taking her eyes off Allen.

Allen sighed. "He won't be the same when he changes."

She stopped. "What?"

"He won't be the same person. None of you will."

Simms looked at me, then back at Allen. He answered the question she didn't have to ask. "I infected you when you grabbed me. It won't be long now." She snatched his shirt again, despite the risk of infection. She put her .45 under his chin. She would blow his brains out; I just knew she would. For the life of me, I didn't want to stop her. "You know I'm willing to die for this," Allen said, finally. "You know that's who we are. You saw it yourself."

She let him go, pushed him against a stack of doorknobs. "You son of a bitch. What the hell have you done to us?"

"It's inevitable. Evolution. Things change, they evolve. Become better."

"Where the hell is Slow Walker?" I asked.

He nodded toward the window. "Probably on his way home to help with the infected there."

"Oh my God." I thought Simms was crying. Simms didn't cry. "You sent him to infect all those people? There's children there."

"It's better this way." He looked at me and smiled. "I changed Slow Walker in the car. You watched it happen, Kid. It made you feel good to be a human being in that moment, didn't it?"

"Fuck you."

"I saw you, saw your eyes. Felt what you felt while you watched me comfort him."

"I thought you were helping a sick man."

"I was."

"You were killing him. Taking his soul."

Allen shook his head as if to disagree, but he didn't say anything. I think he felt as if we were a lost cause.

"Why are they out there?" I asked him.

"For you all. They've come to help you through the transition. It's hard to evolve. You need the comfort, the connection to others to come into second being. That's what it is, you know. A second state of mind—one different from your own. They'll touch you, take just a bit of flesh, but it's simply to become one with you. Your flesh nourishes them, and in return, someone else's flesh will nourish you, and in this way everyone will be connected to everyone else on the planet. We have to do it. We need to. It's why we shake." He looked down at his shaky hands as if contemplating some grand theory. He rubbed them together, touched his face slightly, then scratched just behind each of his ears. The wounds were almost unnoticeable. He suddenly stared at me, as if he had forgotten I was there, and started right back where he had left off: "We have to infect, need it like it's a part of our essence. It's in our nature. You must understand this. But it's better this way. Safer. No more pain or suffering. Because if one person suffers, then all people suffer. No more people dying in the streets for seemingly no reason at all."

I had a thought. "Is everyone in building two infected?"

"Changed, yes." Allen wasn't regretful at all. There were almost a hundred people in that building. I hated him in that moment. I hated everything he stood for. This wasn't human. It didn't matter if they cared more about each other—that wasn't human.

But it was Simms who spoke out. "This is not okay just because you think your own version of good is best. That's not what it means to be people. This is not choice." On the floor, Cadillac Man continued to giggle like a madman. "Shut the fuck up," Simms warned him.

"He's not a threat to you." Allen's temperament never changed. That was more frightening than anything else. To be human was to have emotions—different emotions. It even meant having the wrong emotions at the wrong time. Feeling happy when someone you did- n't like had something bad happen to them—that was part of being human. Not this.

"Who? This piece of shit?" She kicked the man again. Then she just stood, as if contemplating what to do next. She looked at me, but I had nothing. No answers. No witty response. Her hands began to shake.

"I still have control over me. You won't have control over me," she said. I wasn't entirely sure that she was right, and she knew she wasn't either. Once she dropped to the floor, there was nothing to do to change it. Allen was right; it was inevitable.

"Let it happen, Simms. Please understand."

On the floor, Tiny groaned in pain. He was hurting. I could... feel it. I don't know how I knew, but there was something about his spirit that told me he was dying. Allen looked at him, then at me. "You feel it, don't you? He can't do this alone. Let me help him. I can help you all."

"Hell no." Simms pointed the gun at him. "Leave him the hell alone. You've done enough."

"If I don't help him, he will die. Do you want that?"

"Fuck you! Don't make this about me. You did this to him. You did it!"

"We did it for him, Simms. I scratched him, yes, infected him. But I didn't kill him. You'll do that if you don't let me help him."

Simms used her gun hand to wipe the sweat forming on her forehead, and in that moment I thought she was losing her mind. She was so upset. I was worried about what she would do. I think Allen was worried too. She was unpredictable. Finally, Simms turned her anger on the one person she felt justified to harm: Cadillac Man. She pointed the gun at him.

"Don't—" She shot the man in the head, point blank. Allen shook his head. "It's not necessary. Everyone can survive this."

I stared at the two people before me. Thought about what he'd said. I wasn't sure that I wanted to survive it. But what would my mother do without me? My building was depending on me to return. What would they do without me? I couldn't just leave them any more than I had been able to leave without finding out where Slow Walker had gone. I just couldn't.

Then I understand about the lights and why they hadn't just stormed in, changing people. There would be too many losses. The casualties would be too high. They didn't want that. They wanted people like me, like Slow Walker, who would return to their homes to ease the transition. They wanted mules.

Simms closed her eyes. I think she had come to the same revelation that I had. Her hands shook so badly now that she held her gun with both hands. Suddenly, she raised the gun once more, pointed it at Allen, and before the man could respond, she shot him. Outside, the horde groaned, screamed in pain. It was as if they knew he was dead. It would not be long before they stormed the building and killed or changed all of us. I wasn't sure which was worse.

She looked at me. "I can't do it, Kid. I just can't—" There was something in her eyes, and I knew. I just knew that she meant it.

"Simms!" I screamed and ran toward her just as she blew her chin out through her brain.

I stood in the giant one-room store for longer than a moment. Longer than two. Quite a few longer than I probably even remember. I had a choice, contrary to what Simms had said. She'd had one too. She had chosen to die. On the floor, Tiny screamed out in pain. His dark skin had turned an ash grey color, and I knew that he wouldn't make it much longer. He was going to die, and I wasn't sure that I could live with that.

I walked over to the door, opened it, and let a few of the horde walk in. They gathered around Tiny, touching him, nibbling on his exposed skin. One of them lay down beside him, holding the big man within his arms, comforting him in a way that I felt I could never be comforted.

But I decided to give it a try, anyway. I was tired. If this was evolution, who was I to stop it? I was just a stupid kid with one shit of a choice and afraid of change.

CUE: The End. They'll be happy to see me home. I'll bring others. They will help, reaffirm, bring into the fold. I'll be there to smooth the transition. Things will change. I'm not sure if it's a good change or bad change, and that scares me. But it's inevitable, always has been.

I read somewhere that God is Change. Maybe that's true. Maybe it doesn't really matter anymore.

"It is a peculiar sensation, this double-consciousness, this sense of always looking at one's self through the eyes of others, of measuring one's soul by the tape of a world that looks on in amused contempt and pity. One ever feels his two-ness,—an American, a Negro; two souls, two thoughts, two unreconciled strivings; two warring ideals in one dark body, whose dogged strength alone keeps it from being torn asunder."

—W.E.B. Du Bois

"The Room Where Ben Disappeared"

I'd come home to Hatten Hills for the holidays. Christmas was in less than three weeks and I'd been called on for my mother's sake, due to her strange, erratic behavior. Driving into town, I could see that Hatten hadn't changed at all; it was still a small, quaint town that didn't fancy strangers or newcomers. Coloreds were a whole different story, and were, of course, one of the reasons that I had left home more than three years before and had not returned. Even for my father's funeral.

Thomas Thather had died almost a year before. My mother had sent word that he had passed only after he'd been dead and buried for a full month, and so there was no real reason for me to come back. At least, that was what I told myself. But the reason lay within that house on Hatten Hill, deep within the walls of what had been my home for more than twenty years. In that room where Ben had disappeared.

When I drove down Hatten Drive, a road, like the town, that had been named after my family, my motorcar bounced uncontrollably, and it brought back some of the strange feelings that I'd had during my childhood. I began to get the feeling Hatten House was glad I had come home. That it somehow understood I had been gone. I would swear that I heard it sigh. Perhaps, however, it was only the moan of decades of stress. The road hadn't been paved over back then, but it had been, since. A feeling of déjà vu seeded itself deep in my soul, and I could not lose it even as I stepped into the house.

"Young David!" The voice boomed through the foyer.

"Hattie Mae!" We hugged tightly. I had really missed her, probably more than anyone else. Maybe it was because she had been my mother in those days. Hattie Mae was my nanny. She was colored.

"House sure has been quite lonely without you, boy." She giggled, her chubby tummy bouncing like Santa Clause's.

I smiled in spite of myself. I'd sworn that I would not get back into things here. That I would not allow anyone to break through, convincing me to stay on. I couldn't say why, but this scared me more than anything.

"Your mother's in the sittin' room."

I followed her into the room where my mother sat in front of the fireplace, just staring. Staring into the fire almost like...she was somewhere else. Her honey nut hazel eyes twinkled with far away thoughts, memories of something long ago.

"Ma'am?" Hattie Mae called, looking back at me with a pathetic smile that said all I needed to know.

My mother didn't stir.

Hattie Mae avoided looking at me. "She does this sometimes, just stares like that. Like she ain't here at all. Like she's gone to somewhere cain't nobody finds her. Ma'am!"

I walked over and sat on the sofa next to my mother. "Mother?" I shook her arm. "Mother!" I was beginning to think that perhaps she had sat there and died and that the glazed look in her eyes was simply a glimpse of death and nothing more.

"Mother," I said again, and shook her fiercely.

"Hm? What, what is it?" She looked around the room and finally focused on me. "David, is that you?"

She touched my face, and a shock of electricity passed though us. "It's me, Mother. Are you all right?"

"Yes, I'm fine, dear. I was dreaming that I saw your father. We were at the beach. You remember when we use to go to the beach, David? You loved it there."

I nodded my head and took the moment to look her over. She had grown older since I'd seen her last. She looked thin, frail. Her hair had gone almost completely white, and her skin was like paper.

We ate dinner out on the balcony that evening. Hattie Mae had fixed my favorite childhood meal: steak and ice cream. My mother sat rather quietly the entire meal and simply smiled at the right times when I told a joke.

We didn't have much to talk about since we hadn't seen each other in several years, and in fact, hadn't really spoken before I'd gone. My mother and I'd had the typical mother and child relationship for a Hatten Hills family. If you counted that we were well off. *Better than well off,* my father would say, *we were worthy.* Depends on who you asked, if I had to say. Rich didn't always mean better, if you know what I mean. Of course, I never said as such to him; it would not have been accepted.

After dinner, my mother retired to her quiet room. Hattie Mae told me she spent most of her time there now. "Hardly ever comes out anymore," she said. "Talks to no one in there, and sometimes..." She didn't say anything after that, and I didn't push her about it. The less I knew about my mother—the less involved I got in her affairs—the better.

In my room, I put my things away and sat on my bed. Nothing much had changed in there. My pictures of horses still hung on the walls. My blue bedspread with the red and white stripes covered the bed, and my dresser sat lonely in the corner.

I lay my head on the bed and sighed. I'd had a long trip, and the rail-train had been one of the most uncomfortable I'd ever experienced. My bed felt nice, soft and inviting. I soon drifted off, letting my dreams take me where they would.

I dreamed I was falling. My mind whirled along with my body. I fell through times and places that I had never been. I saw things that had yet to be and that I could never have experienced, except in my dreams, but yet I knew them to be true. Decades of past, present, and future passed me by as I tumbled into oblivion. I couldn't say it was a nightmare, as much as it seemed a warning of things that I didn't understand. I saw my mother watching me with my father on the sofa in the sitting room. Both were smiling as if I had made them proud somehow.

I couldn't help but think this was not true; I felt ashamed, but for the life of me I didn't know why.

From the room next door came a loud thump, awaking me instantly. I stood and walked over to the wall. I thought I heard voices, talking in a muffled tone; whispers. I leaned in, putting my head to the wall, and listened. I could hear my mother talking, but at first couldn't make out what it was that she said. Slowly, I began to make out a few words at a time.

Something like, "He loves steak and ice cream. Always has." But her voice was different; it was like it had been when she was younger, stronger.

Then came another voice, and I couldn't quite make out what was said. The words seemed farther away, like talking on the wire to someone in another state.

I walked out of my room and over to the quiet room door. The noises seemed louder there. I distinctively heard a man talking, but still I didn't know what it was that he said. There was a dim light coming from under the door, streaming into the hall. It covered my bare feet, dyeing my toes a pale bluish color.

I knocked on the door. There was another loud thump, and my mother screamed, "Ben, don't run in the house!" I froze; I hadn't heard anyone say that name in two decades. I looked behind me and saw Hattie Mae coming up the stairs.

The voices got louder, almost like everyone was beginning to scream, all at once. But that wasn't it. No, it was as though they were getting closer, as if they were coming from far away and were drawing nearer. I looked at Hattie Mae, and she stared at me, her eyes soft like they used to be when I was a kid.

The light under the door grew brighter and extended longer and longer each time it flared. I had to see who was in there and what they were doing.

I grabbed the doorknob, flung the door open, and jumped in as if I were catching a thief. Inside, my mother sat alone, staring at me strangely.

"What is it, David?" she asked.

Hattie Mae had followed me into the room, and she walked over to my mother, helping her to her feet. "It's getting late, Ma'am. Let's get you off to bed."

I searched the room. No one was there.

Later, Hattie Mae came into my room without the benefit of a knock on my door like she had done when I was a child.

"Good to have you home again, Young David." She wore a checkered handkerchief on her head, and it took me back to a place that I had forgotten long before; a place that I wasn't sure that I wanted to go to again. She smiled and closed the door behind her as she left.

When I finally got my mind to settle down, I dreamed again. This time it was different. It was a memory. A memory about Ben.

But as soon as the sun rose, I forgot what I had remembered the previous night.

The next day, I found my mother in the garden behind the house. Sitting and staring. I was surprised she had managed to keep up the medium-size patch of assorted flowers.

"Did you know that Hatten House wasn't always called as

such?" She spoke without bothering to look at me. "I'm too old now to remember what they used to call it, though. Something like the place that changes you."

"How are you feeling this morning, Mother?"

"Young David, that's what Hattie Mae calls you. You like it when she calls you that, don't you?"

"I don't know. Not really. I haven't really thought about it." It was a lie.

She kept talking, almost as if she hadn't heard me at all. "She was always like your mother. You loved her more than me. I know that."

"No, Mother that's...that's not true." What else could I have said? It was something that had gone unspoken between us for years. We both knew the truth.

"Oh yes. Yes you do. I would see the way you'd hold onto her, when you'd fall and hurt yourself. You were almost like her own. She nursed you, did you know that?"

I didn't bother answering. I figured that she was getting to that age when she looked back on her life and didn't like a lot of what she saw.

"That was all I knew," she continued. "My mother had raised me and my brother that way. But you always had the finest things. And we did the best we could with Ben. You know that, don't you?"

I walked over to her, put my hand on her shoulder. "I know that."

"Do you remember him? He sure watched over you, being a few years older and all. You followed behind him like he was the best thing you'd ever seen."

"I don't remember much, to be honest. Only little things, like the songs." I began singing, lost in the thoughts of the mind of a five-year-old child. "'All around the Mulberry bush, the monkey chased the weasel.' Or something like that; I can't really remember."

"You remember that?"

"Yes. And dogs and something happened. Something bad. What was it, Mother? What happened to him? It was like one day he just disappeared. I think I used to remember, but not anymore."

She smiled at me, and her eyes had changed. She was gone again. "Did you know they didn't always call this Hatten Hills?"

Inside, Hattie Mae broke the green beans for dinner. She sat at the sink and whistled an old tune that I couldn't quite place. My mother had been right, I did have very fond memories of Hattie Mae. Motherly memories. I walked over and put my arms around her shoulder, a gesture that I would have never afforded my mother.

"How's your momma?"

"She seemed fine for a moment, but was not herself the next."

"She's that way sometimes, now." Hattie Mae reached up and grabbed my hand, holding it close to her face.

"Hattie Mae, my mother mentioned something I hadn't thought about in a long time." I paused for a moment, squeezing her hand, not really knowing what to say next.

"What was it she mentioned, Young David?"

"Ben."

She quickly let go of my hand. "Ben? What did she say about him?"

"Just that I looked up to him." I grabbed a raw green bean and put it in my mouth, longing more for something to fill the silence than anything else.

A loud crash came from the top floor. I jump a foot. Hattie Mae stared upward, climbing to her feet. She didn't move as quick as she once had, so it seemed to take her an eternity to get off the stool.

I dashed out of the kitchen and up the stairs. I looked around as something else broke above my head. The noise had come from the sitting room.

Just as I flung the door open, a young colored man stood staring at me, as if seeing a ghost. I focused on him as from the corner of my eye I saw the room change from our furnishings to something of a whole new shape and style. It shimmered a kaleidoscope of colors, moving as I watched. The man himself did not change, although he looked strange in his attire, his head clean-shaven, his clothing new and shoes polished.

But something was strange about him; I felt somehow that I had seen him before. That somehow I knew this colored man, but couldn't quite place him.

Despite my present circumstance, I was not afraid. I was bewildered. I did not feel threatened; I felt curious. My mind raced with answers, and I came to the conclusion that I must be dreaming.

The entire mirage shifted, as if it were a child's toy viewer sliding to a new scene. And then it was gone. The man, the places and images, all gone.

Hattie Mae had not followed me up this time. She stood downstairs with my mother by her side. My mother was my mother once again.

I couldn't control myself. "What in the hell is going on here?" I yelled. "Do you know what I just saw? No, you can't know. Hell, I don't even know what I saw."

"Young David, please sit down. Calm yourself."

I paced back and forth. "You know what I saw, don't you, Hattie Mae? Mother?"

She chewed on her bottom lip for a moment, then slowly began to speak. "Do you remember, David, what happened to Ben?

I shook my head. "I just remember a few things. Smells. Clothing. Songs."

"Let me ask you something." She looked at Hattie Mae and then back at me. "Have you ever walked into the room and switched on the lights and caught something, something that just wasn't quite right? Something that shimmered or moved when you were the only person in the room?"

"That's just the lights playing tricks with your eyes."

"It's more than that, David. Have you ever been somewhere and you're sure that something just brushed up against you, but you were alone?" She paused just long enough for me to think about her questions. "Have you ever experienced déjà vu and just knew that you've done this very thing before, but can't for the life of you know when or where?"

I nodded, not sure where she was going with this. Not even sure that I *wanted* to know.

"Have you ever been in your motor car and caught a ripple of something in the distance, and when you get up on it, it's gone?" She paused. "I say all of this to explain that within this house, within those walls of the sitting room, those things are reality. Something is special about Hatten Hill, and that is why the Indians valued it, and that is why your great grandfather chose it. In that room, David, I can still see your father. And I can still see Ben as a young boy."

"That's crazy... I've...never heard anything so crazy in all my life."

115

"It's true, David. Hattie Mae here can see them too. She can see her boy, Ben."

I was silent. These two old women had lost their minds. Maybe I should have come home and helped out sooner. But right now I just wanted to get as far away, as fast as my motor car would take me.

"Somebody once said that right now is past, present, and future all at once. I think that is true here at Hatten House."

"That's ridiculous." I was a college educated man. A student of common sense.

"Do you remember what happened to Ben?"

"I told you I didn't."

"Try to remember."

"I can't."

She reached out her hand and clutched mine. "Follow me."

She led me up the stairs to the sitting room. I stood outside the door, afraid to open it. "Go on," she said. "It's all right. I've been back there a few times myself."

I reached out, opened the door, and stepped inside. As soon as I did, I began falling. I fell at a rate of thousands of feet a second. Decades of past, present and future passed me by, as if in my dream.

I saw my father's funeral, and my mother's as well. I saw Hattie Mae, who would outlive them all, crying over my mother's casket. I saw a chubby chocolate face smiling as I passed it by, and my seventh birthday—I had just enough time to count the candles.

Then I landed. I was standing in the foyer, but something was different. There it was: the chest that my mother had given away years before. And that picture of the horse that my father kept in his study; somehow it had gotten misplaced over the years.

I became aware of a loud dog barking in the distance. A gunshot rang throughout the room, shaking the windowpanes.

I was there; I was back to the day it had all happened.

At once a young, ebony Ben of about fifteen came running through the front door. He opened it so hard it slammed into the wall, knocking my father's hanging horse picture to the floor, shattering it to pieces. So that was what had happened to it.

As he ran in, my mother and Hattie Mae came from the kitchen to see where the noise had come from.

"Ben, stop that running in the house," my mother had shouted as he ran into the study, where my father was slow to respond. He stood and looked at Ben.

"They. After. Me." The young man was out of breath.

"What?" My father pulled back the window curtain, and I could see several men in the distance with dogs and shotguns. One man held up his gun and fired into the air again.

"Christ," Mother said. "What's going on, Ben?"

Ben had calmed down a bit and was able to speak more clearly. "They said I shamed Dr. Peterson's daughter. I ain't done no such thang, sir. I ain't touched her. I swear it." He put his finger to his heart.

"We know you wouldn't, Ben," my father said. He looked at my mother just as another gunshot was fired, and in those two seconds I knew a decision had been made. My father grabbed Ben's hand and ran over to Hattie Mae and my mother.

"When they come, tell them you haven't seen him. They won't rightly believe you, Hattie Mae, so you'll have to set them straight. It won't hold them for long, but it'll be just long enough."

I remember my five-year-old mind trying to digest all that was happening. It was hard for an adult, but for me... Ben was my brother; that was all I knew.

Father dashed up the stairs with Ben and went into the sitting room and slammed the door behind them just as the men ran in through the still-open door.

"Where is he?" one man shouted, his big brown dog barking loudly. I remember the smell of old dog poop and onions. The other men followed, some with guns, some with bats. Doctor Patterson was with them.

My mother stepped forward. I could see her shaking under her skin, but she didn't back down to them. "What is all this, Patterson? How dare you—"

"Where's the boy? Dogs say he came in here."

"What boy? David's been here all day."

"You know very well who I mean. That nigger boy. Where's he?"

Hattie Mae walked over to the man, ignoring his dog, "What you want with my boy?"

He didn't answer her, simply reached out and slapped her.

Hard. She fell to the floor, and mother ran over to comfort her. She bent to cradle Hattie Mae and shouted up at the man, "Harold Jenkins, you oaf! How dare you?"

The doctor walked over to the five-year-old me and scratched my head. Like a dog, he did. "Hallo," he said. "David, do you remember me?"

I didn't move.

"You go to school with my Carrie. How are you, young man?" He smiled. "Have you seen Ben, David?"

My mother and Hattie Mae looked at me. I felt strange. I didn't know what to do. I liked Dr. Patterson, and he had always been nice to me. And my mother had told me never to lie.

The Doctor stood between me and my view of Hattie Mae, "Did he come in here, David?"

I watched in horror as I nodded my young head. *No!* I hadn't done that. Had I? I didn't remember this at all. I couldn't have done it. *No! No!*

The doctor smiled. "Good boy. Where did he go?"

I pointed to the top of the stairs. All at once the men dashed up to the top floor and began checking all of the rooms.

The thirty-nine-year-old me let a tear fall from his face for the sins that the young David had committed against his family. Finally, the men all gathered around the sitting room door as one man kicked it open. They all ran in and we could hear things being broken up there.

But the room was empty.

When the men had satisfied themselves that the house was clean, they left. My mother walked up to me and hugged me, telling me that I had done the right thing. I remember even then not feeling that this was the truth.

In the end, I did that which I had sworn I wouldn't do; I chose to stay on at Hatten House. I think fondly of my parents; they are not the people who they seemed to be on the outside. I still visit the room where Ben disappeared often. But it's just to sit and daydream. I, like my father, have learned the value of the room. But I, unlike my father, have found no real reason to use it.

Perhaps that is a good thing in these times.

"THE LIGHT OF CREE"

Cree had become a woman exactly five days ago. Twelve years old and already a woman—who knew? She didn't feel like a woman, didn't particularly look like one, with the front of her blouse clinging to her chest like a flat piece of paper. But she *was* a woman. At least, that's what Momma said. And Momma was never wrong.

"You've come on your period, baby."

That's what Momma called it. Period. Which meant that Cree would leak every month like a broken water main. And that was how she felt—broken. Like something was wrong with her. Momma had explained to her that every girl had to go through this, but that didn't matter. She still felt...different. Like something was off. As if she had become a completely different person overnight. But of course, she had.

You're a woman now, she told herself to no avail.

That feeling of change could have less to do with the fact that she had come on her period and more to do with the man she had seen the other day—the strange one.

She had been walking back from the cemetery with her grandmother when she had first seen him. She and her grandmother would go there every so often, clean the stones and pick the weeds.

"We've a lot of people buried here," her grandmother would say. "We gotta take care of 'em. You'll do the same for me, I hope."

"Yes, ma'am," she'd say.

That's when they saw him. A man, perched with both feet on a single fence post, staring at them. A big, wide brim covered his face; a long black coat hung over the post that he crouched on, flapping in the wind. Though she couldn't see his face, she saw his eyes. They were bright, like a shining sun, staring at them from under the hat.

She grabbed and squeezed her grandmother's hand, scared, and the old woman pulled her onward. She wanted to stop, to turn and walk the other way, but her grandmother wouldn't let her.

The man didn't move, his coat swaying and cracking in the wind, his hat shadowing his dark face, his eyes fixed on Cree and her grandmother.

"Keep walking. Don't even look at him," her grandmother said.

"But, what —" Cree started to ask.

"Don't. Don't," her grandmother warned her.

Cree didn't try to talk again. As they reached the man, his head turned slightly toward them. She tried not to notice, but from the corner of her eye, she kept seeing that hat move, almost as if the hat itself were watching them. Once they had walked past, Cree sighed a bit. Behind her, she saw the man's coat flare up as he jumped from his spot on the fence.

Her heart jumped in her chest; she knew he was chasing them. She squeezed the old woman's hand so hard she thought she'd break it, and her grandmother squeezed back, reassuring her. Behind her, Cree could still hear the man's coat flapping as he chased behind them.

She couldn't help it; she had to look. She jerked away from her grandmother and turned to face the man. She wasn't going to let him attack her from the back, and she wanted to see his face. She didn't know why, but she had to... to show him...

But he was gone.

She scanned the woods from side to side, but could see no trace of him. The wind had died down a bit, and she tried to listen for his footfalls in the woods, but she could hear nothing.

He was gone.

She couldn't get that image out of her mind—him standing there on the fence, staring at them through no eyes at all. It scared her, even now.

"What was he?" she asked her grandmother.

"A Dark Man," the old woman said. "A memory."

"A memory of what?"

"Of that man. His own memory of himself."

"You mean he was dead?"

"Yes, baby, he was dead. He's lost, like... like in those woods there." She pointed to where the man had come from, her finger shaking. It shook because she was old, not because she was scared, Cree knew. "Remember when you was little and you got lost in Cavanaugh Woods? Remember how scared you were, and you thought you'd never get home? Remember?" Cree nodded. "And your brothers found you in the barn, crying. You weren't very far from home, but to you it might as well have been a million miles away." The old woman paused, looked at her. "That's how it is for him. He's right there, but cain't find it home."

"To heaven?" she asked.

"To heaven, baby." Her grandmother bent down, her knees creaking from the weight of old age, and looked into Cree's eyes. "Sometimes, sometimes, they need a guiding light.

"You're special. Cree. I've always known it. Since the day you was born with that caul covering your face. The veil of sight and knowledge. That's why you can see him. That's why he can see you. You must come of your own soon, and find your own way."

Now that Cree thought about it, perhaps they did relate to each other—seeing this dead man and becoming a woman. After all, she had seen him for the first time the day she'd come on her period, hadn't she?

"You know what this means, don't 'cha?" Cree's friend Karen asked her.

"What?"

"You're a woman now."

"I wish people would stop sayin' that. I ain't no woman."

The girl laughed, her round face lost in her dimples. "Now you gonna go get fat. Start eatin' up everthang. Get all moody and mad at everybody for no reason at all."

"Why would I do that?" Cree stared at her reflection in the pond, her dark skin smooth and youthful in the crystal color of the waters. She thought maybe she'd see something, any hint of her womanhood. Nothing.

"I don't know. That's what happened to my sister; at least that's what my brother said. He said she was painted."

"You mean tainted?"

"No, he said painted. Thought he was being funny. You know, like...red." The girl looked at her, serious. "They say this thing can change you. That it hurts sometimes. Makes ya do strange things— *see* things."

Cree nodded, not saying anything. She *had* seen things, after all. Strange things.

"You ready for tomorrow? The water's cold this time of year. When he throws you in, it's gonna seem like you're down there forever. That's what Joe Ann said."

"He's my daddy. He won't leave me down there long."

"I hope not." Karen put her arm around Cree's shoulders. Cree shuddered; she couldn't help it.

Today she would be baptized. Brought to the Lord. At least, that's how Daddy had put it. *And he won't leave me down too long.* She was sure of it.

Not only had she become a woman only a few days ago, but now she would become a Christian, too. Boy, how time flew. Now was the period—poor choice of words—of cleansing. That wasn't what Daddy said, but that was how she felt. Like they were washing away sins that she had yet to commit.

Not long ago, the pains had started. They began as throbbing sensations in her belly and raced up her back to her spine. "Birthin' pains" was what Momma called them. "Crawl-into-your-bed-and-never-get-out-again-pains" was what she called them.

Would this ever stop? She asked her momma how long this period thing would last, and her momma said that it would be her close friend for the next fifty years.

Fifty years! Would she even live that long? Cree wasn't sure, but with a friend like that, who even wanted to?

The pain moved from her stomach and raced up her back and kept pounding that sin into her somewhere in between. She just wanted to lie there and die. She waited in her room, in her white gown, her hair combed and braided into four tight plaits on her head with white bows tied at the ends. She sat on the bed, staring out the window.

Toochie walked into the room, wearing her Sunday dress, and sat on the bed beside her. "Nervous?"

Cree kicked her short legs back and forth and didn't answer her sister.

"Don't be. It's not that bad. Daddy just says a few words, dunks you, and that's it. Everyone'll be watchin', but that ain't no big deal."

"He doesn't hold you down there long, does he?"

"No. A few seconds. Just long enough to wash that sin away." Toochie laughed.

"You sure?" Cree wasn't all that sure it was funny.

"Yep. I wouldn't lie to ya, now would I?"

The sun was shining and coming up nicely, the orange and red light spilling into the room, bleeding onto Cree's toes. Toochie had polished her toenails just for this occasion: auburn.

They wouldn't be having regular Sunday services today. No, instead everyone would be meeting at Muller's Creek, so as to see her baptized. They had done it for her sisters and all of her brothers. In fact, they did it whenever the time came for a child in the church to come of the Lord.

Her father stood in the lake, the water up to his knees. He didn't bother to roll up his pants, either. He never did; just stood there in his Sunday best, wading in the water.

The rest of the congregation stood off to the side. Wide-brim hats for as far as she could see, dark faces staring at her, smiles adorning the faces, as if they were so proud to be bringing another soul to Him.

Daddy reached out his hand to her. She walked over to him, the icy water making goosebumps appear on her skin. She couldn't believe how bitter the sensation was between her toes, of all places. The sun had yet to reach its peak, and the pond was still hidden in shade. When the water reached her ankles she almost cried out from the cold.

Then Daddy grabbed her hand and all other thoughts faded away. It was so soft, so soothing. He had a way of making everything seem okay, as if nothing was allowed to hurt her when he was around.

The man pulled her close to him, smiling. He looked so proud, his long face not showing a hint of his age. He whispered to her, "Don't be afraid. I'll hold on tight."

And she knew he would, too. He would hold onto her for dear life and never let go. Her pulse, which had begun to race a mile a minute, slowed to a simple crawl, and she smiled back at him, trusting him with all her heart. All her mind; her soul.

He spoke, more to her than to the gathering crowd. "We've all come here to witness your rebirth. Now shrouded in darkness, a symbol of the life of darkness you're leaving behind, you shall come into the light..." The words were drowned out, not by the water, but by her mind. They went into her ears and got all mixed up in her head. It wasn't that she couldn't understand him. It was just that she was too nervous and excited, all at the same time, to focus on the words. They were foreign to her.

Suddenly, he dunked her. Water enclosed her face as she fell backward into the pool. Her eyes, nose and mouth became surrounded by water, and her ears drummed from the rushing coldness. Underneath, she felt a sense of wellness, almost as if what everyone else had said was true: all of her sins were washing away in that water. Everything was great. All was well. She felt happy, good.

For a split second, Cree opened her eyes. A bright light radiated around her, and she saw her daddy's face staring down at her. She was surprised that the sun had risen so high and that it now shined down on her. The water around her heated, and she relished the warmth.

She continued to stare into her father's eyes through the murky water as his smile suddenly turned into a look of concern. The light grew brighter, and she realized that the glow was not coming from the sun as she had previously thought, but from her.

That's when her grandmother's words rang back into her ears. *Sometimes. Sometimes, they need a guiding light.* And in that moment she felt that her grandmother had been talking directly to her, as if somehow the old woman knew. Perhaps it was true. Perhaps her grandmother had been speaking to her, warning her. No, as Cree thought about it, she didn't feel the words were meant as a warning, but instead as a guide—just for her.

A guiding light.

A revelation came to her, as suddenly as the water rushing over her body had. She didn't know where the thought had come from, but she didn't question it; it was simply how things should be. She thought: *I am the light.*

The light was within her. It was a part of her. She was a part of it.

You're special, Cree, the old woman had said. *I've always known it, since the day you were born with that caul covering your face. That's why you can see him. That's why he can see you. You must come of your own soon, and find your way.*

Slowly, she rose as she felt her father's hands guiding her back to the surface. Her feet reached the ground, her hands still at her sides. She felt great; she never wanted this feeling to end.

Cree stood on her own two feet as the water ran down her face and the air reached her nose again. She breathed.

She looked over to her father and realized for the first time that he was not holding her. In fact, he was standing far away from her, toward the edge of Muller's Creek. She had been holding herself— coming of her own.

Everyone was staring at her with strange looks on their faces. And *he* was among them.

The Dark Man. The one she had seen with her grandmother when they were walking from the cemetery. He was staring at her, too. His eyeless sockets fixed on her, as she thought again:

I am the light.

The guiding light. Those words sprang to her mind as the revelation dawned upon her. She knew now what she must do. Just as the sun rises, brightening a new day, so, too, must the Light of Cree.

"THE TEACHINGS AND REDEMPTION OF MS. FANNIE LOU MASON"

They came for her, this time, as they always had: afraid. People's fear drove them to do irrational things, and she was usually blamed. Fannie Lou Mason didn't think most people were evil; in fact, if she had been asked right at that moment, she would have said they were simply scared. Frightened people lashed out—against her.

"Come here, damn you." The man dragged her out of the house by her leg, leaving the bag with her herbs hidden somewhere within the house. The crowd gathered around her and stared. None of them bothered to speak out for her, as she knew they wouldn't. She had only been in this town for a few weeks—just about the time the rain started—and there was no one to speak for her.

It had rained for fourteen days without stopping. One Friday morning, the skies had opened up, flooding the land, killing the crops. A young boy had drowned in the rapid rush of the nearby river, and more children had gone missing, thought to have also perished in the deadly torrents. It was not within her power to save these children. She had come for a different reason. Now she hoped she could at least save herself.

Fannie stood, mud caked to her dress and slip; she looked at the man before her. Samuel Pickens had come to her only days before because he was in love with a married woman in town. He wanted her to hex the woman and send her his way. Fannie had told him she didn't do that kind of work. He hadn't been happy— nothing had changed in those few days. Samuel spit tobacco onto the ground and chewed, a big wad gathering in his cheek.

Fannie closed her eyes, held her face to the sky, prayed. Quietly, she mumbled a few words, verses from her books. The rain continued to pour into her face and into her mouth while she spoke. She paid no attention to it. Her voice rose louder and louder, rising above the heavy rains.

Another man walked up, grabbed her. "Stop this. What are you doing?"

Slowly, she lowered her head, looked into his eyes. "Praying."

"For what?"

"You." She surveyed the crowd. No one had moved to help or hurt her. They were afraid, not dangerous. "All of you."

Tears welled in the man's eyes and he let go of her. The water had slowly risen and was covering her ankles. Her dress was completely drenched, the hem floating in several inches of water.

Sara Mae slithered through the crowd of people until she reached Fannie. She was a short and dark woman with dark eyes. Her son was the boy they had found dead at the shore's edge. She touched Fannie. "Please, make it stop."

Fannie shook her head. "I can't. I'm sorry."

"Yes you can," someone screamed from the back. She didn't know who had said it. As she looked on, she was sure that the crowd had gathered to over a hundred people. Most of them just stood, watching the event. They simply wanted answers. She understood.

Almost the entire town had come to her. Every man, woman and child. Good. She had prayed. She had prayed.

"Help us," someone else shouted. She never understood how people knew who she was, but they always knew. Most of the time she didn't try to keep it a secret. She regretted that she couldn't do what they wanted of her. She wanted them to realize that.

After a moment, at precisely 7:34 p.m. Fannie Lou Mason knew, a loud noise broke the sky, echoing throughout the night. The entire crowd turned toward the small town hall from which the noise had come. They were about a mile away, but it was downhill from that point, which offered a spectacular view of the township. Suddenly, there was a thunderous cracking noise that sliced through the silence. People screamed and children clung to their parents. Everyone watched as the crudely made town hall building shook from the wet, unstable earth beneath its floorboards and tumbled to the ground. The groundwater and rain rushed in, taking the pieces away to the nearby river.

Slowly, things began to calm down, and every face turned to her, eyes questioning, sad.

"You couldn't be in there," Fannie said.

Samuel Pickens spoke first. "The town hall meeting. First Thursday of every month."

She nodded.

He said simply, "We may... I was so angry...we could have... hurt you."

"I know."

From within the crowd someone screamed; the sound shocked

Fannie Lou. She searched the group of people, mentally taking note. Something wasn't right. She couldn't quite put her finger on it, and so she scanned them again, until she realized what was wrong.

Oh, no. Fannie Lou pushed her way through the crowd, counting everyone, each face, every man, woman and child. *One...two... ten...* She had to account for every person. How could this have happened? She had been so thorough. She had done her job. She pushed several people aside as she made her way through the crowd; the people simply stood, staring at the shell of a building. *Twenty...forty... Please, please, not this, not now.* She wanted to scream, yell at everyone to get out of her way; what in the hell was wrong with them? Why were they not helping her? Something was wrong. She had...*done* something wrong.

Sixty-eight, she silently counted out as she reached the woman who cried while she pointed toward the ruined building. In the distance, the water and rain washed away the final remains of the destroyed structure. Sixty-eight.

There should have been seventy-two people.

Fannie Lou looked at the woman, afraid to meet her eyes.

The woman spoke: "I sent them on before me, told 'em I'd meet 'em there. I didn't want them to be here." The woman seemed disconnected, out of her mind. "I didn't want my babies seeing what we'd do to you."

2

Three years later...

The Lord wasn't as generous to the Negro folk as he was to the white man. And many years after Fannie Lou Mason saved the people in that small town somewhere in Virginia, the same could still be said. Most didn't feel God was biased; if you asked white folk, they would simply say that they were the better race and so God had blessed them; if you asked Negro folk, they would say that because they were last on earth they would surely be first in heaven and were therefore the chosen people.

But where most agreed were the twin baby girls born to Walter Kelly and his uppity wife. Indeed, the Negro children—one was bright as day and the other dark as night—were both quite beautiful. Even a

blind white man, it was said, could see that. There was just something about them that one couldn't put into words, and most didn't
try. They were different and it scared people. Fannie Lou Mason
understood very well the attraction of the sisters. She had kept an
eye on the girls for a long time, and now she watched from the back
pew, unnoticed.

Somewhere along the way, Leona and Iona had grown up to
become lovely young girls—among whispers of good or bad things;
Fannie Lou wasn't sure. But at the age of nine, they had grown to be
intelligent, powerful young ladies. She could feel it even through the
rhythmic pounding of the church choir. The woman, who had just
arrived the previous evening, watched the girls, trying desperately to
be inconspicuous.

The children's lives, as with so many children, in so many
places, in so many times, were lived in a rushed bubble of field
work, trips to the fishing pond for swimming and hidden places and
secret joys. They lived with their mother and father and three older
brothers.

Church was one of the places that most attended out of a sense
of misguided loyalty—the girls seemed to feel the same way. Fannie
Lou closed her eyes, slowed her breath, trying to connect with the
girls, see their thoughts, their inner feelings. The twins, not surprisingly, were also connected, each feeling the emotions of the other.

What she felt was that neither of the girls could say that they
hated church, per se (after all, who would say that?) but they didn't
like having to sit all day in that small, stuffy one-room building. Iona
swung her legs back and forth, kicking the back of the rickety
bench. Only a few years before, her feet had barely been long
enough to hang over the sides. But now she relished her newfound
freedom and swung with gusto until her daddy gave her the look,
which probably meant she had better stop, or risk getting taken out
back to the woods for a whopping.

Fannie Lou breathed slowly and looked to all of the world as if
she had simply fallen asleep there on the pew. However, she was
completely engulfed in the emotions of the girls. It was so refreshing
to feel something other than the usual wearisome-ness associated
with adult life. No, instead, these girls had freedom that the woman
envied. She sank deeper into them, their youthful thoughts.

Then a succession of images flooded her head:

Iona, the youngest of the girls, stared at Mrs. Davis as she shouted an "Amen," and Leona giggled, knowing that before long the woman would be wiggling in her seat and would fall to the floor, shouting crazed hallelujahs to the Lord. Their momma always said the woman's antics were all for show and that the spirit didn't come that much to one woman, especially a woman like that. Fannie Lou would probably agree with her. Beside Mrs. Davis, a man waved a brightly colored fan with a picture of a pretty white angel on the back, over her. Mrs. Davis's daughter, who was expecting something the girls could never quite figure out, simply stared forward, ignoring her mother.

The twins' oldest brother, Jacob, covered Leona's mouth with his hand to keep her from making too much noise. Mr. Jefferies bit off a great big hunk of his tobacco, chewed on it a bit, and got up and spit in the tub in the back of the church. He winked at the girls on his way back to his seat. Above their heads, something buzzed, but none of them seemed to pay any attention anymore. Bees had gotten into the rafters a while back, and some of the menfolk had flushed them out. Now, everyone just pretended that they didn't hear them up there.

Finally, when the preacher was finished, everyone got up and shook hands "in fellowship." The girls seemed to shake everyone's hand in that room at least five times. Fannie Lou opened her eyes, rose to her feet, and followed the crowd outside into the bright daylight. Several people watched her, pointing, but she paid no attention. By the time she had made her way outside, Iona and Leona were already there, whispering with each other.

Mrs. Davis' daughter wobbled out, taking each of the stairs one at a time. Her feet were as big as sausages, and her belly was bigger than her head. She strolled by Fannie Lou, right past the girls, smiling at each of them, and walked off into the trees and disappeared. Iona looked at Leona and then back at her parents, and before her sister could stop her, she dashed off into the woods after the girl. Leona followed, her bright skin flushing red in the heat. Fannie Lou was right behind.

It was so much darker inside the tree line than it had been outside. The sun hardly peeked through the bushy treetops at all, and if she hadn't known better, the woman might have thought that it was actually nighttime. Just as Fannie Lou walked into the tree line, she heard a girl crying in the distance. Her cries echoed off the trees, and it sounded distressed. Somehow, everything seemed to distort in those woods—everything was so foreign. Fannie Lou walked just close enough to hear, but she knew the others had no idea she was there. She preferred it that way for now. She simply watched.

Iona turned to her sister, Leona, and Fannie Lou got the over-whelming sense that something was wrong. The oldest twin seemed not to like that feeling—it probably hurt her. Made her feel as if there was something that she should be doing but couldn't. Fannie Lou understood this feeling. Leona tried to stop her twin from go-ing, but the younger girl pulled away from her and walked up to the pregnant woman.

The young lady sat on a fallen tree trunk, her hands perched on top of her massive stomach. Tears stained her face, falling to her humble dress in fat drops, staining that too. She tried to smile when she saw them, but it was strained. Leona seemed to be struggling to remember her name, but Iona looked at her sister, and as if reading her mind, nodded and said, "Janice." They did that sometimes—knew each other's thoughts, Fannie Lou knew.

Iona made her way to the girl, "Are you all right?"

"Yeah." Iona touched her. Janice jumped as if shocked and looked into the older girl's eyes.

"How old are you two now? Nine?"

Iona nodded.

"I thought so. I remember when you was born. They say you two was special, ya know." She paused for a long time. So long Fan-nie almost thought she'd fallen asleep with her eyes open. "It hurts...real bad." Janice touched her stomach and moved her hand between her legs. "It ain't time, though. I got me two months to go. It's somethin' else. I can feel it."

"I know," Iona said. When she looked at the girl, Fannie saw something in Iona's eyes flare up like a light. It was calming and warm, as if it were a fire burning to temper Janice's soul. Leona stood back for a while, as it seemed to scare her. Janice stared at Iona, and after a while, closed her eyes.

Iona spoke: "Suffering never last as long as it feels sometimes. And heaven come after, Momma said. So it's worth it, I guess." Fannie Lou smiled. The girl was quite powerful, indeed.

Janice smiled, nodded. She sat there for a moment longer, then stood up and wiped her dress clean. When she walked away, she was just a little lighter on her feet, her back just a bit straighter. Fannie knew her pain wasn't gone; instead, she was sure that Iona had made the young woman just strong enough to bear it. Iona had touched her soul, she knew. Their gifts were so strong. Perhaps, Fannie knew, too strong; they were not contained. She had to save these girls, or the town from the girls. She hadn't decided which.

"It's dyin'," Leona said to her sister, completely unaware of Fannie Lou's presence.

"You sure?" her sister asked her.

Leona was sure—Fannie Lou had seen it too. The two had seen something Iona hadn't. Something that no matter how long Leona lived she would never forget. There had been something in that girl's belly, crawling, wiggling around, alive, smothering the life from the baby.

She'd seen worms.

3

The previous Saturday night had brought rain and torrents the likes that Colored Town, Kentucky had not seen since either of the girls were born. It also brought Fannie Lou Mason. She was a tall, thick-waisted woman who wore skirts that were way too short and showed her ankles and part of her legs. She was lofty and black, thin and shapely. There was something about her eyes that people commented on and that made them instantly wary of her. She didn't have a northern accent or a southern one. There was nothing noticeably discernable about her, and yet she called for attention.

As the story goes, on the night she arrived, Fannie Lou got out of her crude little horse-drawn buggy and said simply, "Colored Town, Kentucky, you pray for me." Then the woman knelt down on all fours and kissed the ground. She grabbed a hand full of dirt and let it slip slowly from her fingers while the wind and rain blew it away.

As the rain poured, she lifted her head to the sky and let the water wash over her; she smiled. People watched. She didn't acknowledge them, seemed not to even notice. Colored Town, Kentucky was a place only worth mentioning if you were leaving it on your way to somewhere bigger and better. The people kept to themselves and didn't want to get in anyone else's business and expected the same. She understood this.

After a moment, Fannie Lou walked over to a tree, caressed it with the tips of her fingers. Kissed it. Then, she tore off a small piece of bark, placed it in her mouth and chewed it, slowly, deliberately.

Hoodoo Woman. The word had gotten around by the following evening.

4

Nine-year-old Leona Kelly ran through Cavanaugh woods with her twin, Iona. She was ahead of her sister by only a few feet, which was how they had come into the world—one right after the other. Just as her foot stomped on a leaf, sinking into the moist land, behind her, her sister caught up, her tiny feet crunching on the same dead leaf moments later. The woods, the trees, and the soil smelled fresh from the moist early morning dew, and the air was thick with fog and moisture as steam rose from the earth.

They were inseparable—as they had been since they were born. Momma always told them, "Girl, you didn't cry until you had seen your sister safely on this side." They didn't really look alike, Leona being several full shades lighter and her eyes being blue instead of brown, but they *felt* it, down inside. Something linked them together like a fence enclosing land, keeping everything that didn't belong out, and making sure that everything that did, stayed inside— that was what they did for each other.

They were linked in other ways too. They had always been able to know what the other was feeling, and they had both seen things, strange things, since as long as they could remember. The girl closed her eyes for a brief moment as a woman with a broken face and an apron with a pretty red apple on it flashed though her mind. She squeezed her eyelids tighter and tried to wipe the thought from her mind.

Leona looked back and saw her sister smiling at her, her dark face cast in shadows. Iona was smaller, and when she was born she had almost died. She had only been five pounds, and Daddy said that he could hold her whole body in one of his hands, and she had gotten only taller since then, he'd say. She was still a beanpole with arms and legs and eyes, he'd laugh.

The girl tripped, and before she could catch herself, she had fallen down. Leona ran to help her up. Iona sat in the dirt, rubbing her knee. "It's not that bad," she said to her sister.

"Let me see." She had just scraped it, but Leona doted over her anyway. She knew she was the oldest, and if something happened, she would be the one getting a whopping, even if it wasn't her fault and she was only older by a few minutes. That was simply how it was.

She helped Iona up, and they walked the rest of the way, Leona supporting her sister with her own weight. The trees were dense in that part of the woods, and they were both glad to just feel the other close. It was always so dark here; it was the only place in the world that, even when the sun was high in the sky, remained part of night's domain.

Somewhere in the distance, through the break in the trees, they could see the light of day, so they walked steady. The house sat off in the woods, to their right, in the deepest, darkest, remotest part. Some place off in the distance, a loud bird squawked, and Iona trembled beside her—and the two girls laughed a little for their fool-ishness. The house wasn't far from them, and they loved to play there when no one else had time for them. Momma had lived in that house when she was little, before they had moved out and someone else took it over. No one really owned it; it was there, like many other old shack-houses in those parts, for the taking when someone *needed* it. But now the roof had fallen in certain places, and when it rained, half of the house flooded with water. A dirt line crossed the inside about halfway up on the walls where the water would rise during a flood. The bushes had grown and covered the front windows, and you couldn't see in or out of the house.

Iona's knee was feeling better. She pulled away from her sister and walked up the front steps, watching each stair closely, as there were big holes that could swallow a whole person. Leona followed slowly, skipping a few stairs that were particularly bad. They weren't supposed to be there, so if one of them got hurt, not only would they have to be left there while the other got help, but they were sure to get a whopping when they got better for being there in the first place.

The porch wasn't much better than the steps, so they eased

across it and in through the missing front door. It lay off to the side somewhere, within a heap of trash and discarded things from the previous owners.

The house was stale and musty; too many floods, and too long it had sat being uncared for and forgotten. There were memories here, the girls knew. They felt them in every brick and board, in every shingle, as it smothered them and surrounded their senses until they couldn't remember anything else but what the house had once been, and that it had once been a proud building, standing strong for the family it kept—and the family that kept it.

They made their way to the closet door, overlooking the piles of trash and dangerous debris everywhere. Since she had been the first in the house, Iona opened it, as if she thought something was waiting inside to pounce on them at any moment. Her sister came over to join her. Inside the abandoned closet, a pile of old, dirty shoes lay, not one of them with a match. Shoestrings lay tangled and wound in knots as if they hadn't been touched in years.

The two worked meticulously, undoing the knots until they were all loose. Leona handed her sister a few shoes, keeping several for herself, and they made their way to the bottom of the steps, sitting down with their backs to the wall opposite the staircase.

The girls took turns throwing the shoes up, hitting the bare wall at the top of the stairs and rolling back down again. Each girl threw and each watched her shoe roll back down again. This was fun; if one of the shoes stopped and landed on the stairs, the other would try to hit it, knocking it back down again.

However, every once in a while, the shoes would not hit the wall and come rolling back down to them, but would go over the side and into the upper, deserted region of the house. And this was the really fun part.

That day, Iona was the first to have her shoe miss the mark, landing in one of the back bedrooms. The two watched the shoe fly through the air, twirling, twirling until it disappeared into the darkness. They sat there for a few seconds, waiting, watching. And as they expected, within seconds, the shoe was thrown back down to them. It flew from the top of the stairs by unseen hands and rolled back down the steps, bounding one slow stair at a time.

Iona looked to her sister, and the older girl smiled a bit, a little frightened and a little excited at the same time. They knew no one lived in the house, and they knew if they dared to go up the stairs, there would be no one up there. But still, something threw the shoes back down to them, every time, without fail. They weren't really afraid; they'd been doing this long enough and had even done it with their brothers when they were little.

Something rattled up in the darkness of the house; something moved as if walking from one end of the room to the other. Outside, everything remained still and quiet. Leona threw the shoe, the dirty string twisting as it flew. Darkness overtook it before it landed somewhere out of sight. After another moment, nothing had happened and it did not come back to them. She stood up, thinking perhaps their game had come to an end, but just as she did, the shoe came twirling through the air, hitting her on the side of the head.

She let out a loud scream, grabbed her sister and dashed toward the door—behind them, footsteps banged down the stairs, chasing them. Careful not to trip, the girls jumped off the porch, skipping the stairs altogether, and ran until their little feet wouldn't take them any farther. Behind them, the door slammed shut, and the last remaining shutter fell to the ground as the house rattled.

The girls stopped. Leona bent down, holding her knees, out of breath, watching the house from a safe distance. They burst out in nervous laughter while making sure to keep an eye on the front door to ensure it didn't open again. Beside her, Iona was out of breath too, her heart racing. The girl took her hand as they walked away, Leona feeling her sister's heartbeat through her palm. Their hearts pumped blood together, through identical lungs to separate bodies that had each once been a part of the other.

This, in fact, was the most important part—feeling the rhythm, the life of the other, feeling as if they were one again. It was so much stronger now than it had been only a few months ago—they felt connected in a way they never had. They sighed, relishing it.

The girls knew that when they returned, the shoes would be back in the closet, the laces knotted as if they hadn't been touched in years, waiting for them to throw them back up the stairs into the unknown depths of the house that their momma had once lived in, and which now stood abandoned and unwanted by everyone but them.

"How can you be so black and your sister so pretty?" asked

Eddie Gray, who was twelve, and three years older than she was. He was so dumb she thought that God had etched it somewhere on Eddie's mind with His great big pencil so that no matter what the boy did, he couldn't be smart.

"I don't know," she whispered. The question did have merit, and as much as she hated to think about it, she had asked it to herself more times than she could count. She never got an answer.

"What was that? You don't know why your sister's so much prettier 'an you?"

She shook her head. Iona didn't know what to say. She never did when people said things like that to her. She didn't know why God had made her so black and her sister almost white. She had never thought about it until she had gotten old enough to know what color meant. And black wasn't no good color at all, she reasoned. Because if it was, then people would be trying to get black instead of putting so much powder on their faces so as folks would think they was lighter than they was. Her momma and daddy wasn't yellow, like her sister, and neither were her brothers; she just guessed the girl had gotten lucky.

The boy laughed, and somewhere in the back of her mind she wanted to go to him and hit him upside his nappy head. She didn't like him. He made her feel like she wasn't good enough or something. But she didn't hit him—her daddy had taught her better than that; girls had to behave themselves.

"What's going on here?" The new lady, Fannie Lou Mason, walked up and stood beside Iona. She placed her hands on the girl's shoulder.

"Nuthin'."

"Nothing, huh?" She looked at the girl, then at Eddie. "Didn't sound like nothing to me. What you doing here picking on a girl half your size?" She walked up to the boy, stood only inches from him and a full foot taller. Eddie Gray stared at the ground as if ashamed of himself or scared of the woman, Iona wasn't sure which. "Well, you better get the hell away from here, boy. 'Fore I skin your ass redder than a rose." Iona had never heard a woman saying bad words before, but she thought she liked it. Before that moment, Iona had never really thought about it. Girls didn't say that kind of thing. And they didn't wear dresses that showed their ankles and part of their calves. There was something strange about Fannie

Lou Mason, and Iona liked it.

Eddie didn't move; he was frozen scared. Then the woman hollered, "You hear me, boy? Don't make me knock your ass. What are you waiting for? Get!"

Anger flashed in Eddie's eyes, and he looked at Iona as if he could hurt her. Then he ran away, his head still hung low.

The woman walked over, held Iona's face to her. "Hold your head up. Me and you ain't too different, you know. Both in a world that don't appreciate us." She giggled a bit, winked at her. "We have to stick together. Me, you, and your sister. We're the unwanted, but they need us, you know."

5

To be honest, as soon as Fannie had seen the girl, Janice, at the church she had known that the young woman would come to her. She just hadn't expected it to be this soon. Before the girl had arrived, the night had been very pleasant. Fannie Lou had taken up lodge with a couple she had never met, the Warrens. But they were allies. She had them scattered around the country and they put her up when she needed or helped when necessary. Tonight was necessary.

Outside, the wind blew thick raindrops against the old shack, rattling the planks as warm air seeped through the holes in the walls. As far as Fannie Lou was concerned, the wind was more than welcome on that humid night, as was the cooler rainwater that blew its way in through the cracks of the humble shack. Somewhere in the distance an owl made himself known to the world and to Fannie.

The man of the house sat in his chair, smoking the one pipe he said he allowed himself per day. The woman was reading her Bible. She read it every night before she went to bed, Fannie Lou knew. They were like many other couples in many other places all over the world—these people just chose to make a difference. She respected them for that.

Then someone banged on the door, ruining the peace. The woman jumped, dropping her Bible on the floor. She quickly picked it up, kissed it, and held it to her chest. Fannie Lou smiled. The woman put a lot of faith in her "good book."

The knock came again, louder, more urgent, and Mr. Warren went to answer it. The old man didn't bother asking who it was. He

knew the only people who came this late at night were there because they had to be there to see her.

Janice stood in the doorway, rain soaking her through and
through. Her belly was bigger than a girl her age seemed able to
carry. She stared at the ground as if she thought it would speak for
her when the time came. It didn't. When she looked up to meet
Fannie Lou's eyes, she seemed worn and broken down from something heavier than that child in her belly.

"We ain't got no doctor here," Mr. Warren told the girl.

"I don't need one," she said. She looked back to Fannie Lou.
"You her, ain't'cha?"

Fannie Lou nodded. They both knew why she'd come.

The girl rubbed her stomach. "I got me a heavy load here.
Birthing mother said everything's fine. But it ain't, I know it ain't. I
can *feel* it." The rain weighed on the girl, and Fannie Lou caught a
glimpse of her face as lightning cracked above her head. She walked
onto the porch, and warm air swirled around them as they stood
there surveying each other. The girl didn't really seem frightened,
but that didn't surprise her. By the time people realized they
needed to come see her, they had long passed the point of fear.

"What's your name?" Fannie knew her name, but she wanted
to get her attention, make her concentrate on something other than
her problems. But Janice didn't seem to hear her, so Fannie Lou
asked her again.

"Janice."

Fannie nodded, looking into her eyes, seeing her trouble. That
was her way. No one ever came right out and said what they thought
was wrong with them. If they named it, then somehow that would
give it credence. She knew this to be just as true as anything else.

Janice was content to stand on the porch with her. The young
woman looked down at her belly as it moved a bit under her dress.
Fannie Lou thought at first it had just been her imagination, but as
she watched, it wiggled as if a nest of snakes lived just under the
girl's dress. Janice stared at her stomach, then into Fannie Lou's
eyes.

Without warning, Fannie Lou reached out and laid her right
hand on Janice's belly. She pulled the girl to her, her palm caressing
the hard, swollen stomach. Janice's skin bubbled beneath Fannie
Lou's hand, almost as if it was boiling from her touch. The girl's

eyes were closed, and Fannie Lou thought for a moment that she had passed out. The lightning came again, exploding through the night. Thunder broke the sky for the first time, the boom resonating throughout several counties, Fannie Lou was sure.

Inside the house, Mrs. Warren had set some water to boil on the stove, sensing the baby might be coming. Her husband simply watched from his chair, smoking on his sweet-smelling pipe. Fannie Lou didn't acknowledge any of this; her hand and her mind worked on the child—a boy, she sensed—and its mother.

She grabbed the girl tighter, sending a wave of power through her body, into her womb. The child kicked once, but something was stopping it. Something was filling the girl's belly, suffocating the child, keeping it from moving. Fannie squeezed the young woman's stomach as hard as she could as she gathered all of the energy within her and shocked Janice through the tips of her fingers. As she did so, the lightning broke through the roof of the porch, where the two stood, striking both Fannie Lou and the girl. The force sent the two soaring backward.

Janice landed in the yard, the wet earth breaking her fall. Fannie Lou flew into the house and slid onto the rug, her butt scraping on crude wooden floorboards, her dress flying above her head, showing her bloomers. Outside, the girl crawled through the grass and up the steps, her belly almost dragging the ground. Mrs. Warren ran into the night to help Janice back to her feet. Inside, Mr. Warren helped Fannie Lou up. The old man looked at her, his face somewhere between fear and wonder.

Meeting on the porch again, Janice grabbed Fannie Lou's hand and placed it on her belly. Fannie Lou could *feel* that the things in there were agitated and circling the child as if it was their food source. Rain tumbled down on the two through the hole that the lightning had left in the overhang of the roof. The planks had broken, leaving an opening in the porch floor big enough for the two to fall in. Looking as if they were locked in a dance pose, Janice taking the lead, they made their way around the porch, sidestepping the massive hole.

She had to help the girl, she just had to. There had been a time, several years ago, that Fannie hadn't been able to save both the child and mother. She couldn't let that happen again. She was stronger and more powerful now. She could do this.

The things inside the girl were strong, and Fannie Lou felt over-whelmed with hopelessness and a vileness that she had not felt in a long time. They seemed to feed from the child, she knew, but they were also taking their energy from the mother, from her grief and fear. They ab-sorbed the souls of the two, like parasites. Fannie Lou's hand began to change. The skin began to wiggle, moving up her fingers, through her hand and then her elbow. Her body trembled as the vermin squirmed their way through Fannie's body. She was used to taking on others pains and changing them, using them for good. But this was different.

This was not good. How had these children been so strong, so powerful?

Janice saw her hand and screamed out, grabbing Fannie's arm with her own small, dark fingers. She wasn't scared of the worms, as Fannie thought she should be. Instead, Janice seemed as if she feared that she would infect Fannie Lou. "Not her," the girl screamed, squeezing Fannie's arm just at the elbow, staying the vermin.

Fannie Lou's fingertips tingled as the power ignited in her again, and she sent a shockwave through the girl. Janice's body trembled and convulsed as Fannie Lou sent another strong bolt through her. The third time, the two broke apart, and Janice stood there staring, her eyes as wide as saucers.

From beneath her dress, a trickle of fluid poured down her legs. At first, the girl seemed not to notice, but as she looked down, a massive flood fell from within her womb to the porch landing at her feet. Maggots and worms wriggled on top of each other, seeking a new host, a new home. Blood and thick mucus mixed as things unnamable moved, some crawling up the girl's legs or out onto the porch toward Fannie Lou.

"Get out of the way," Mrs. Warren screamed. Fannie Lou grabbed the girl and pulled her free of the mess, just as the woman poured the pot of boiling water onto the mound. Steam rose from the porch in waves, and the things melted into the cracks, sizzling away. A few strays inched in different directions, but Mr. Warren caught them with the broom. When he was finished, he swept the remaining mess into the yard, threw the broom out on top of it, and set it afire with gasoline from the shed.

The girl still clung to Fannie Lou as the fire blazed, the rain having no effect on it. After a long while, she asked, "Will my baby be all right?"

Fannie nodded. She thought perhaps it would. She had a good feeling about it. Mrs. Warren came and got the girl after that and led her into the house; the old woman had coffee on the stove and had boiled more water so the girl could take a hot bath.

As Janice entered the house, she turned to look at Fannie Lou. Then, as if for the first time, she took in the full damage to the house. "I'm sorry. I didn't mean to... I can pay you. I..."

"No need," Mr. Warren said. "We make do here." The girl started to say something, but then closed her mouth. His tone said that he would hear no more talk on the matter.

Fannie Lou stayed outside for a while longer, staring at the fire as it finally began to die down, and then back at the house, where the simmering mess was little more than froth covering what was left of the porch.

She closed her eyes, knowing that she would doom the twin girls to a life such as this. But she had no choice. If their gift remained unchecked, there would be more like Janice, more people suffering from the weight of the girls' uncontrolled burden. Leona and Iona had no idea what they had done to this mother and child— if Fannie didn't teach them, they would continue to negatively affect the people around them until they learned how to control themselves.

Fannie sighed. They were cursed, just as she was.

6

Colored Town was a small place in northern Kentucky. It was a thriving town of Negro people. So far, they'd been lucky because they weren't near any large white communities that could blame them for anything that went wrong, or when the whites just wanted to blame someone for their troubles. For the most part, Fannie liked it here.

She rounded the corner, keeping the twins within sight. The girls, hand in hand, scanned store windows as they passed through town square. Finally, they stopped at the goods store.

Inside, while the girls looked through fabric at the back of the store, Fannie took the opportunity to buy a few items for the Warrens—some yams, corn, and turnips—and herbs she needed. Most of her herbs, Fannie found in the wild. They were always fresher, and she didn't like people asking questions about some of her particular choices.

When she finished, she paid for her items and went outside. Soon afterward, the girls came out of the store and headed home. She would stop them on their way home—there was not time to waste. The girls needed to understand the danger they caused for those around them. Leona and Iona walked through the wooded area toward their home, and Fannie stalked slowly behind until they were completely out of sight of town. She didn't want to scare the girls, but for the life of her, she felt like a predator stalking prey. Perhaps, she realized, she was.

Just as she called out to the girls, a man walked up from behind, startling her. She wasn't the only predator in these woods today.

"Well, as I live and breathe, Fannie Lou Mason. I done heard you was here."

Fannie looked at the man, and although he looked familiar, she couldn't place his face. She had known a lot of people over the years; too many to count.

While she watched him, his half smile turned to a frown. "You don't remember me, do you?"

For the life if her, she didn't. She could feel the contempt radiating from the man, but she didn't know who he was. He hated her. She stared for a moment longer, and then it came to her. "*My God,*" she whispered, "Steven Pace." A memory flashed through her mind:

It had been more than ten years before and Fannie had only been a child herself, just out of her parents' house. She had been called to the Pace farm. They were good people, but had a heavy burden with six mouths already to feed. Alma Pace was birthing their fifth child. They wouldn't have called the young woman at all if the oldest daughter, Samantha, who was barely fifteen, had not gotten frightened from all the blood and sent her father to get Fannie.

Fannie had been known around town to save a baby if the time ever came for it. She was young and didn't know much about her abilities at that point, but she was usually capable of helping sickly children. After all, she had saved the Butlers' child, who was almost two months early a few months before, and the boy was healthy and strong as an ox now.

As Fannie entered the house, the first thing that struck her was the silence. She had delivered a lot of babies in her time. The young woman had never really wanted to do it, but they always called on her, and who was she to refuse? It was her duty to help her neighbor. And in all that time, the one thing she could always count on in a birthing house was noise. Either it was the mother screaming her head off because the pain was so bad she didn't think she could take it, or it was the people moving around the house trying to get everything in order for the new baby. But there was always noise.

The Pace house was chillingly quiet.

When she had ridden up, the entire clan had been standing around the porch. The children had stared at her as if she were the chosen one come to save their kin. Their father, Steven, had helped her off the wagon and ushered her into the house. For the life of her she hadn't wanted to go through that door. She was not chosen, she was not a saving grace. The broken, creaky boards had seemed to not to want to hold her weight, but they had held, making every step loud and painful to her ears. The hole in the roof had been patched more times than even she could count; she had seen Steven in the goods store buying material for it not long before, but still there was a bucket under the massive hole to catch excess rain water and dew from the frosty mornings. It was probably used as some of the family's drinking water.

Inside, Samantha tended to her mother, wiping her forehead with a wet cloth and checking every now and again to see the process of the child that would soon enter the world. The second-oldest daughter—Fannie couldn't remember her name—paced in the corner and only came out when her sister called on her.

As soon as Samantha saw the young woman, she seemed to sigh from within. Fannie knew the feeling. She had seen it many a time. If something went wrong, people tended to blame the first person they could. Even if that person had been there to help, and had done the best they could. Blame was an inevitable part of the process. Anger had a large part in it too, but she understood. How could she not? People always needed something to hold onto, and rage and anger were just as good, if not better, weapons as anything else.

Fannie walked over to the girl, who looked so much smaller in that room. She would be having a husband and family of her own soon, but so help her, Fannie Lou could not but see the child in Samantha's eyes. She was frightened.

She looked at the girl still standing in the corner. "What's your name, child?"

The girl looked around as if she thought the young woman could be talking to someone else, then she touched her chest. "Ma'am?" Just then, her mother grunted, clinging to her stomach. A large amount of blood poured from beneath her gown and soaked the bedding. The girl jumped back as if struck and stared at Fannie, chewing on her forefinger. Fannie knew the girl would be no good in that room.

"Your name, girl. What's your name?"

It took her a moment before she figured out she needed to answer, and when she did, Fannie could barely understand her. She had said something like "Sadie" or "Sandy."

"Okay. Why don't you go outside and sit with your brothers?"

"But..." The girl's eyes were wide. "But, don't you need me to help?"

No, I don't need you, Fannie thought. She did not need someone who looked like she was going to fall into two pieces if you looked at her wrong. She needed someone there who could be of use to her. Someone more strong-willed. But she said, "I think your brothers may need you out there. Think they may be scared. Why don't you take care of 'em, for me."

The girl was relieved as she threw down the dirty cloth in her hands and ran out the door. Behind her, the screen slammed and the loud bang comforted Fannie.

She looked at Samantha. "Are you all right?" The girl nodded. "Okay, now go and get me some old rags. Lots of 'em. Make sure they's clean as possible." The girl dashed toward the back of the house.

Fannie stared at the woman. "Is the pain bad?" Alma had had her eyes closed the entire time Fannie had been in the house, but Fannie knew the woman was awake and listening to everything that had gone on. The woman nodded her head, her eyes still closed. Alma had probably been calm for her children's sake.

"We got some blood here. It's too thick." The woman didn't say anything. Fannie got up and washed her hands in the water bowl and came back. "I'm going to take a look over."

Suddenly, the woman opened her eyes, breathing hard. "Sadie's a good girl." She took several more breaths, blowing through clenched teeth. "She's just timid sometimes. She's scared to death of mice and bugs and everythang. She'll be all right, though. She'll be all right."

Alma seemed to be talking to herself, so Fannie ignored her. She moved the woman's legs apart and felt inside her. Alma squirmed a bit, but didn't cry out. Fannie knew this was probably painful. But Alma had birthed four children before this one and knew what to expect. The woman had not had this kind of trouble before, though. All of her births had been easy compared to this one.

Inside the woman, the cord was knotted and tight around the child. Fannie tried to move the baby, her hands slipping over the moist body. But the cord seemed to tighten even more.

Samantha came in with several strips of cloth. The girl had just torn several of them, jagged threads trailing behind her. For the most part, they were clean and unused. Fannie used several of them to clean up as much of the blood beneath the woman as she could. The others she put aside for the child. Either she would need them to keep the baby warm or she would need them for a shroud to bury it, but she would need them.

Alma screamed for the first time since Fannie had been in the house, and the noise scared her. Alma bent over, clutching her belly, trying to feel a child growing weaker within her. Fear rose in Fannie Lou as she realized she might not be able to help the mother and child. She thought she feared more for Alma, as she had several more children still left to care for.

Alma was losing too much blood. The rags were drenched in dark crimson, but most of the blood was in a puddle on the chinkapin oak floor beneath her. The wood, which was used in most of the houses in the area, was stained, and Fannie didn't think it would get clean again. It would have to be replaced. She knew the family couldn't afford it, so the blood would stay as a reminder of the day.

Beside her, Samantha cringed as Fannie reached into the woman again, trying to free the child. Tears formed in the girl's eyes, but she did not let them fall. Alma passed out from the pain, her eyes fluttering wildly beneath her eyelids. This meant she wasn't pushing anymore, and Fannie wondered if the contractions had stopped altogether. Things didn't look good for her. She might not make it even if Fannie could get this child out of her.

Samantha didn't need to see her mother die; no child needed to see that. "Samantha, go outside and take care of the others."

The girl's eyes pleaded with Fannie. "Let me stay and help you."

The young woman shook her head. The girl walked out, peeking over her shoulders every couple of seconds.

Finally, Fannie made the choice. She grabbed hold of the child's head as tightly as she could and pulled it out, cord and all. Liquids gushed out with the baby, and she could barely tell that it was a human being at all.

The umbilical cord had wrapped itself around the child's neck. She tugged on the cord again, and the afterbirth slipped out. She packed Alma with several of the clean rags and wished she hadn't sent the girl out so she could wake her mother up and give her lots of water. Fannie hoped that would slow down the bleeding.

She worked on freeing the child from its binding. The cord was tight, and the child's healthy pink color had turned blue-grey. She carefully unwrapped it, starting with the legs and then the body. Just as she began to free its neck, someone placed a hand on her shoulder. She had been so involved in what she was doing, she had not heard him walk in.

Steven squeezed her shoulders. She thought at first he was trying to reassure her, but then he reached down and stayed her hand. It took her a moment to realize what he wanted, and when it finally dawned on her, she wanted to scream.

He stared at his wife and said simply, "If I lose Alma, I don't want it."

"But...she may not..."

"If she lives, I can't afford to feed it."

Fannie's own hands seemed to age right in front of her face. She stared at the child, then at the man. What did he ask of her? She understood his dilemma. It was hard feeding a family, especially one as large as his—and what if he lost his wife? Fannie closed her eyes, sighed. She opened them suddenly. This is not the person she was.

Fannie Lou ignored the father of the child in her arms, continuing to work to save her. After a moment, she freed the baby girl from her binding and tried to clear her breathing passageway.

The little girl cried, though it was weak. Fannie continued to work on the mother, but she could not help her. The woman died while Fannie saved her baby.

Fannie stared at Mr. Pace through the fogginess of her memory. She had almost forgotten about Pace and his family, not because they weren't important to her, but because she had made so many choices since her time in his small, humble home. The man continued to look down on her, and for a split second, she sensed that he was afraid of her. This wasn't unusual; most people who knew Fannie eventually grew to fear her. It was inevitable. The problem came when people's fear grew into rage and then into violence, as it would now.

Right on cue, the man said, "I won't let you hurt another soul." He reached out and grabbed her arm, pulling her body closer to him. She struggled, and he twisted her arm; the pain radiated up to her shoulder. Her face was so close to his that his sour breath spilled over her.

"Who do you think you are to forget me?"

Fannie realized now that he wasn't just angry; he felt justified. Fannie opened her mouth to scream, but it choked in her throat. She looked around—not only were they too far from town, but the only two people who would hear her cry for help would be the twins, and they would be more at risk than she.

Pace twisted her arm, bending it to her back until he stood directly behind her. He took this opportunity to put his hands around her throat, squeezing, caressing her neck until she couldn't breathe. Her arms thrashed back and forth. Finally, she reached behind her, grabbed a large chunk of flesh, and clawed at it with her nails. The man cried out and threw her to the ground.

Fannie fell, coughing, trying to catch her breath. Steven Pace held his broken face between his hands, blood streaming between his fingers. After a moment, he looked at her, fuming.

She held out her hand to stop him. "Don't."

"I'll teach you never to do this to another man, you Hoodoo bitch."

Fannie closed her eyes. She had known men like him before.

She did not belong to this man—she did not belong to any man. Her teacher had died long ago. She didn't need another.

Fannie touched her hands to her chest, feeling her heartbeat slow, rhythmically. As she calmed herself, her breathing began to match her heartbeat until her entire body had become one force, one powerful force of energy. Pace continued to talk and threaten, but she no longer heard him; she had become one with the Earth. Fannie heard the beat of the Earth's heart within its core. Just as she was sure she had melted completely, becoming one with the land, Fannie removed her hand from her own heart, placing it on the earth. The ground began to shake, the dead leaves trembling like live snakes hid beneath them.

The man stopped and looked at the ground. Fannie pulled the energy from inside her body into the ground. A huge chunk of earth shot from beneath the leaves. Debris, small twigs, dirt, and dried vegetation flew like missiles toward Pace. The man was pummeled by the rubble, which knocked him backward. He flew into a tree trunk, his head slamming against the bark, and then slid to the ground between the roots of the tree.

Fannie rose to her feet. She felt energized, clear-headed, excited. She walked over to the man. He tried to stand but fell, dazed and confused. He pointed to her, angry, his mouth quivering. He didn't speak, but his message was clear; he wanted to get up to harm her. Fannie looked around, found a thick tree trunk, and hit Pace one good time over the head with it.

She didn't kill him, she knew, but he would be sore in the morning. Perhaps next time he would think twice about his behavior.

The scarred man, whose wife had died under Fannie Lou's care, woke up in the woods, still angry. The following day, he spoke to the minster about the dangerous Fannie Lou Mason.

7

June bugs led Iona and her sister through the woods by strings tied to their long, hairy legs. Every now and again the bugs would change direction and head back toward the girls and they would run screaming away from the tiny green creatures. The bugs buzzed their disdain, flying high toward the treetops, until the strings reached their length and they fell earthward again. Neither of the girls liked tying the bugs up, and so their brothers would always do it for them. They were so loud, and ugly and green, and their leathery wings looked like they belonged on pendants that some of the church ladies wore pinned on their dresses. In fact, Iona could swear that she had seen Mrs. Margaret wearing one several Sundays before.

The bugs led them past the shack with the old shoes hiding somewhere in a closet, each girl giving it a wide berth while keeping a careful eye on it. They were never really scared of the shack, but they respected it—as their father told them they should respect everything. They knew what could happen to people who didn't respect the things they should. They had seen it.

Somewhere in the distance a cow mooed and grazed. Several more joined the first until there was a low cacophony of their mooing music as the backdrop to the forest sounds.

Baskets, three of them, lay discarded like trash, off in the bushes somewhere—the girls had forgotten where they had put them. They had all but forgotten that they had been sent out to get all of them delivered by sunfall. If they hadn't returned by then, Momma would send Seth and Jacob out to find them, and if they weren't hurt or something, then Daddy would skin them good.

Iona remembered once when she and her sister had played out in the clearing on the other side of the Muller's creek and had lost track of time; before they had known it, it had been so dark the girls couldn't see their hands in front of their faces. They had grabbed a hold of each other and guided each other toward home. Iona had fallen and cut her knee open on a sharp tree root, and by the time they had gotten home, Daddy and the boys had gone off looking for them. When he had gotten home, he had been so relieved to see them that he'd almost forgotten to be mad. Almost. He had taken Leona out back and tried his best to take a layer of skin off her behind. He had yelled at Iona, telling her she'd be next when her leg got better. Lucky for her, it had taken so long that Daddy had decided not to bother. Not *forgot,* he told her, *he never forgot.*

Still, the June bugs buzzed on strings just above the girls' heads, darting this way and that, just trying to get free of their bonds. Their wings were slowing down, and Iona thought that they were getting tired, losing their wills. She had seen them get so upset that they just dropped dead right there at her feet, the strings falling limply to the ground. She supposed that they, like everything else, couldn't live if they were chained.

"Let's let 'em go," she said to her sister.

Leona shrugged and slowly pulled the string toward her, biting through it as close as she could to the leg. Iona did the same. They stared as the bugs flew away and joined the others in the sky heading toward Muller's creek. Leona grabbed Iona's hand and they stood there for a moment, both thinking about things that little girls in big open fields with lots of fresh air think about. After a while, the girls grabbed their baskets and headed off.

They still had three more deliveries before they could go home. The baskets weighed a ton, which Momma said was good because that meant that some people was kind enough and well-off enough to give to others. But they weren't so heavy that each girl couldn't carry two.

Momma, Missus Davidson, and some of the other ladies in church had been doing this for three years now. Twice a year, during the summer and the dead of winter, they would get together and give those folk who weren't as well-off as they were as much food and goods as they could spare. All the church and mostly all the colored folk around gave something, whether it was some dried meat, or jarred food, or an old sweater that their little ones had grown out of. Everyone gave something.

They had already delivered the basket to the Lady Abigail who lived by herself except for all of her cats. Iona thought she had somewhere around a dozen of them, running around all over her and eating whatever they pleased. She had even seen the lady feed them from her own plate. Her basket was always the lightest; the lady didn't eat much. In fact, Momma said she was going to sit in that house and waste away.

Now they were at the house of Widow Robinson and her six young 'ens. The girls took the steps one at a time because they didn't like coming here much. Widow had lost her husband two years before to another woman and her husband's rifle. The widow didn't like taking charity; she said she did a just fine job feeding her family as it was.

"What you want?" the woman yelled through the torn screen door, staring at them like they were bringing the plague, instead of food. "I done told yo momma, I don't want nothin' from her."

The girls looked at each other for a moment. Leona was ready at any moment to leave with or without the basket, her sister could tell. Of course, if they came back with the basket, they would get in trouble and Momma would probably just send them back anyway, so they might as well just get it over with now, Iona thought.

"Ma'am," Iona said, "it's just some jarred food and homemade bread and sweaters and stuff for yo young 'ens." She paused, and when the woman didn't say anything else, she decided to keep going. "I wore one of these sweaters last year, and it kept me *so* warm. It got too small for me a while back, though."

"I don't want no charity from those people. Thumbin' their nose at me." She burst through the wooden screen door, letting it slam back on its hinges. "Makin' me and my children feel like half people 'cause of my husband."

Leona jumped back, but Iona just stared into the woman's eyes. "Ain't no charity, ma'am. Ain't none of us got nothin' to be thumbin' our noses down at. No ma'am, we just wanna help."

"Help? Help!" Her eyes were wild. "I outta knock you one good, girl, ya hear? You ain't got no business *helpin'* nobody." She rolled her head as if she couldn't control it. "You and yo momma and that no-good Peggy Davidson ain't got a pot to piss in and they wanna help me." She laughed like a drunken man. It wasn't a pretty sound, and it didn't make the woman look pretty either.

"Ain't no harm in wantin' to help nobody." Iona's eyes twinkled a bit, and she smiled, and Leona thought her sister had never been so beautiful. The girl walked over and sat on the swing. Leona was sure it couldn't hold her. "I liked him. He was a nice man—he used to give me and Leona penny candy. You used to be able to get six for a penny at the market, and some of yours were babies, so he'd give 'em to us. You remember, Leona?" The girl nodded, scared to say anything when Widow Robinson looked at her.

The woman stood there for a moment, not sure what to say. No one said anything good about her Joe anymore; they only talked about the bad now. The gambling and chasing women. They didn't care what kind of man he was anymore. She looked down at her bare feet.

Iona continued. "And he used to help Daddy sometimes, I remember, with the farm. He did it 'cause he wanted to help us. Do you remember? He wanted to *help* us."

The woman, who Leona could tell had once been very beautiful but now just looked worn and used, nodded her head. Iona knew that her speech had changed, ever so slightly, to match the woman's. This made the widow feel more comfortable, Iona knew, and it made Iona feel closer to the woman. She didn't like talking to people like she was putting on airs, the way her momma sometimes did. Instead, she preferred to connect to them personally. She had a way with people like that.

"Ain't no harm in it," she said finally. "Helpin' folk is what we is here to do." Iona got up, as the swing creaked its protest, and walked to the woman. "Ain't no harm in it, Widow. None at all." She reached out and touched the woman's hand—instantly a shock went through the pair, and the old woman shook just a bit. Then Iona reached out to give the woman the basket.

They both stood there for a long while, Iona's hands outstretched, holding the basket, the woman not wanting to take it. Iona's hands shook a bit, as this was the heaviest basket of the lot. It took a lot to feed six children, and it took a lot to carry the food for them. Iona's little body didn't seem strong enough. But it was.

After what to Leona seemed like forever, and even she had given up, the woman took the basket, her eyes still downcast. Iona smiled.

As they left, the widow called to them. They turned to look at her.

"A good man," was all she said.

"A good man," Iona nodded.

Good man, they heard her say again at their backs.

8

"But I would have you know, that the head of every man is Christ; and the head of the woman is the man; and the head of Christ is God. For the man is not of the woman; but the woman of the man. Neither was the man created for the woman; but the woman for the man. Corinthians eleven, three through eight." The preacher spoke to the crowd, his voice ringing throughout the room. He read word for word from his Bible, finally looking up after a moment. "You see, she is not your master, but you are hers. You are to lead, because she is of feeble mind and body and prone to wickedness. It is God's law, so it must be man's law. You can not deviate from this, or you shall be punished." He looked around, eyeing each person in the room.

Reverend Gregory always preached about wickedness, but it was usually confined to what would happen if people didn't follow God's law. This was different, and he was never this loud. The man almost seemed angry, as if some wrong had been personally committed against him.

"If you don't heed His law, things happen. Our very church, people. Our own church has been infected. Infected with evilness, wickedness. We must root it out, get rid of it." Beside Iona, the twins' mother moved uncomfortably in her seat. She looked at the girls' father several times, and he returned her gaze.

"A woman must wear enough clothes to hide her nakedness. She must conform to the true meaning of being a woman, less she become a witch..." And there it was. Iona peeked around her bench and stared at Fannie Lou's skirt. It looked even shorter while she sat down, her legs crossed. The preacher continued, "Thou shalt not suffer a witch to live. Whoever lieth with a beast shall surely be put to death. He that sacrificeth unto any god, save to the *Lord* only, he shall be utterly destroyed. Exodus twenty-two, eighteen through twenty."

Iona knew that if she understood what the preacher meant, then everyone else in the room did also. It would certainly not be lost on the people that they had a woman of questionable character in their midst. But a witch? What did the man mean by this? Why did he call her that, and what had she done to earn that title?

The man walked down from his pulpit—which he only ever did when he wanted to make an important point—and stood right in front of Fannie Lou. He was not looking at her, but at everyone else. He was quiet for a long time. He had left his book on the podium; this part, he had memorized. "Let the women learn in silence with all subjection. But I suffer not a woman to teach, nor to usurp authority over the man, but to be in silence. For Adam was first formed, then Eve. And Adam was not deceived, but the woman, being deceived, was in the transgression. You see those that obey her are doomed, just as Adam and his apple."

After the service was over, people gathered and whispered to each other. Iona and Leona didn't really want to know what they were saying, so they walked into the woods, just out of sight. Iona thought about the implications of being a witch and what you had to do to become one. She could tell that her sister was thinking about the same thing. She dared not to think what she had already thought: what did this make her and her sister?

While the two sat quietly, not speaking to each other, the woman who had caused all of the trouble walked up to them. She smiled and put her hands on her hips.

"Interesting service, huh?"

The girls didn't say anything. Iona looked around to make sure no one saw them talking to her; then, she was instantly ashamed for being so afraid.

"Don't worry, they won't see."

"I'm not—" Iona tried to protest, but she stopped herself. It would have been a lie.

The woman frowned. "You don't know me, do you?"

Both girls shook their heads.

"I see." She looked up to the sky, eyes closed. Iona thought at first the woman was praying, but there was something so delicate and personal about the way she held her head to the clouds, something intimate. She envied the woman, for a split second, for her freedom. She didn't seem to care what the preacher had said about her. But Iona was simply afraid to be seen with her. How had this black woman become this, now?

Slowly, Fannie Lou lowered her head and looked at the girls. "I am here for you two. I traveled a long way to find you. And I have a lot of things to teach you. Those people in that room are afraid. They've forgotten their history, and now they're afraid of it. It scares them because—"

"Leona! Iona!" their father called from the edge of the woods.

Leona answered quickly, "Be right there."

"I have so many things to show you. But we have less time than I thought. Find me when you're ready. It has to be your choice."

"Why'd you send those chillen to shame me?" The woman confronted Momma after Sunday service. Momma simply stared at her like she had lost her mind—and at this point everyone in Colored Town thought that Widow Robinson had. *She went mad after that old cheating man of hers left her alone to raise all those good-for-nothing chillen,* that's what Missus Davidson had whispered to Momma one day. Momma didn't say it, though; the girls never heard her say anything bad about the woman. Iona supposed that she didn't really have to.

"You ain't got no right to bother me."

Momma shook her head and finished hanging the sheet on the line. Iona handed her the clothespin. Leona stepped back, not wanting to get in the wrath of the woman—she was scared of the widow, Iona knew. When Momma was done, she turned to the woman. "Ain't no shame in givin' to other folks."

"You give to *other* folk then. I don't want yo help, ya hear?" The widow's hair was wild on her head, and she looked like she'd just been sitting there festering since the girls had left her house the day before.

Iona didn't think that Momma could reason with her when she was like this. It happened almost every six months. Every time, Iona would talk her into letting her take the food for the widow's children, and every time, the widow's pride would make her mad that she couldn't offer it to them herself. So she'd come a-marching and yelling at Momma.

"It's for those chillen. Don't eat it if you don't want to. It'd be a shame, there's some good jarred peaches in there." Momma licked her lips.

Widow Robinson was by far the most stubborn woman Iona had ever met. She had tried hard, over and over again, to *work* on her. To help her and soften her heart, if just a bit, so that there wasn't so much anger there, but the widow wouldn't listen. Like an old dumb sow, she wouldn't.

Iona was mad. How come when people wanted to help other people they couldn't just let them? Did that woman know that lending them that food helped them feel better, too? Didn't she understand that sometimes folks didn't give just so they could get back somehow, but because it made them feel good inside?

The woman would know that if she'd just stop being so doggone stubborn.

Iona hadn't realized it, but she had made a sound under her breath, and now both women stared at her. She had to say something, so she did. She told the—not so old in years, but way too old in the heart—woman just what she thought about it.

"Momma was only trying to help. We don't want you to feel bad. She wasn't trying to shame you, Lord knows she wasn't. It just makes her feel better to help other folks. Makes her feel like she's doing something good, something the Lord wants her to do, is all. Ain't no shame in that."

The widow didn't say anything for a long time, but when she looked at Iona, she hadn't softened any. "You ain't no bad girl. You ain't. But you got to understand somethin' too. You take away people's dignity when you give 'em thangs they ain't near 'bout asked for. You ain't got no right. None." The woman shook her head, her hair bouncing around like a wild mane of a lion. "People have the right to feel pride about themselves, and you and yo momma ain't got no right to take it away."

Iona hadn't really thought about that. She had only seen and been told that it was the right thing to do to help others, and so she did it, and didn't think about anything else. She didn't know what to think now. The woman had the right to say no to people when they gave her things. But her children had the right to eat whenever they were hungry. Iona knew that if somebody else were to come and leave them food every month and expect them to just take it, her daddy would get mad. Just like Widow Robinson.

Iona supposed she hadn't really seen the widow as a person, now that she thought about it. Not really. She had just seen her as the widow who needed helping, and so she should be happy just to get that help. Maybe everybody else saw her that way too, and that was what made the woman so mad. Maybe she, like everybody else, wanted to keep something for herself. Some bit of pride, some dignity.

Finally, Iona spoke. "I'm sorry. I didn't understand. I see... I think I see now why you're so mad at people."

When she finished speaking, her momma was angry, she could tell. She thought she might even get a whopping when the widow left, but she didn't care. That was what she thought. That was how she felt. She didn't want the widow to feel alone. Nobody should have to feel like that.

"Maybe I can come and see you sometimes."

The widow got ready to protest, but Iona stopped her. "Not to bring you stuff, but maybe as a friend. Everybody should have a friend. Don't you agree, Widow... I mean, Ms. Robinson?"

The woman looked at Iona, and then at Momma. Iona thought the woman didn't want to hurt her feelings. That was a good sign; a moment ago she wouldn't have cared one bit.

Leona came up and held her sister's hand. The older girl was shaking some, but no one would have noticed by just looking at her. The two girls stared at the woman, and so did their momma. The widow's eyes were wide and wandering all around them, not really focusing on anything or anybody. She looked to Iona, and then at her momma, and her expression changed from soft to hard just that fast.

"Just stay away from me is all I ask. My chillen eat, and they have stuff to wear. Just stay away."

Iona sighed. She would have so liked to be the woman's friend; she supposed her hatred for Momma overruled everything else. Iona could see the pain the in the woman's eyes.

The girl understood.

But there's a funny thing about hatin', her daddy had once told her when she had gotten so mad at her brother that she had said she hated him and wished him dead. *It ends up hurtin' everybody, even you.* She supposed he was right.

The thing was, she knew, come this time next year, her momma would send her back to Widow Robinson's with a big basket of food, and it would start all over again. She guessed that was how life was; people did what they did, for whatever reason they did it, and never really learned anything.

Well, not Iona. She had tried as hard as she could to make the widow better, happier. But it hadn't worked. If she couldn't even help the people who really needed it, what good was it to be able to help them in the first place? Now that Iona thought about it, she wasn't sure she wanted to help anyone. She thought about Fannie Lou and the way the minister had treated her, the way the people of town talked about her behind her back. Iona didn't want that. She didn't want to be that woman. She wasn't strong like Fannie Lou.

She couldn't be a witch.

9

Behind Iona, Leona swung from the vine of a great white oak tree. The trunk was massive and took up a good portion of the clearing that it inhabited. Leona swung wide, bent her little body forward, and jumped from one hanging vine to another effortlessly. Any other time, Iona would have been right there with her, swinging in the wind. But not today. She felt like something had kicked her in the stomach and knocked her flat on her butt.

But she couldn't help feeling like something was wrong. She kept thinking about the new woman, Fannie Lou Mason, and what the minister had said to them. How he had all but said she was evil. The girls had heard the rumors: *Hoodoo Woman.* That's what people called Fannie Lou Mason.

Iona and her sister had talked about what the woman had said, and neither of them really knew what to do. They figured their momma and daddy wouldn't want them to go and see Fannie Lou, but they both really wanted to do it, although they both admitted they were scared. They felt connected to her but they couldn't explain why.

Ever since the girls had been young, they'd both seen things. Things that others didn't; things that their mother and father had told them weren't there. Like the headless Indian woman who roamed the woods sometimes, carrying her screaming baby on her chest as if it were stuck there by mere will alone, suckling on her milkless breast. The woman had reached out to Leona, touching her with dead hands. Leona had never told Iona what the dead woman had done or what had happened, but Iona knew it was something bad.

After that, the girls hadn't talked about seeing anything again. They found it easier that way. If they pretended not to see them, then usually those things just went away. It was almost as if acknowledging the dead gave them power, and so the girls simply denied them. Maybe that had been a bad idea.

Iona looked up sharply into the distance. At the same moment, Leona's gaze was drawn to the same spot. There was something out there, calling them. Iona could feel it in the pit of her stomach, pulling at her. Calling, beckoning her. Leona stood up, pointed. Iona wasn't sure she wanted to know what called them. They'd had these feelings before, but they were usually able to ignore them until they went away. But they had never been this strong.

The two girls walked to the other side of Cavanaugh Woods, following their guts. They weren't usually allowed to play on this side of town because it was a long way from the house. The closer they got, the more the feeling became overpowering. Eventually, the girls came to an open field with a white house stuck right in the center. The house was old; the shingles were falling off, the paint faded.

They had been led to Thomas Fuller's land. As they made their way to the clearing, just beyond the tree line, Mr. Fuller's house came into sight. Mr. Fuller was nice, Iona guessed, but he didn't like folks messing on his land too much.

Iona pointed toward the house. "It's coming from in there."

Leona shook her head and held her sister's hand. "I don't wanna go. We're not supposed to be here, anyway. We can just go home. Pretend nothing happened, the same way we always do. This is no different."

Iona looked down from their slightly elevated position at the house. "This is stronger. Can you feel it? It's different."

"I don't care. I just want to go home."

Iona let go of her sister's hand and began walking down the hill toward the house—the basement, she knew. She looked back to Leona and motioned for her to follow, but the girl didn't move. It was a bad idea to stand right there on the hill; Mr. Fuller would see them if they stayed too long. Leona watched the house, afraid. Iona understood how she felt; she didn't want to go either. But there was something—someone—who needed them. She knew this now. She understood it, even though she didn't know how or why she understood it. Iona stood in the clearing so that anyone who happened to look could see her, and waited. Behind her, a dog barked in the woods, and she near about jumped out of her skin.

Finally, Leona came out of her daze and ran as fast as her legs could take her toward her sister. Just as she rounded the corner, she ran into someone. Iona watched as her sister collided with the person and fell to the ground before she could stop herself. The shape was tall and imposing, and as Iona watched from the clearing, she had no doubt they had been caught by Mr. Fuller.

She was only slightly relieved when she saw that it was Fannie Lou Mason.

Leona bounced off the woman and landed flat on her butt in front of her.

"Shhh." The woman motioned with her finger, helping Leona to her feet. "You felt it too? It's strong here."

Fannie Lou looked around, scanning to make sure no one was watching. Then, the woman bent down and opened the cellar; the doors made a loud creaking noise, echoing through the still day. Iona quickly checked to make sure they were still safe; she was sure there was no way that anyone within a mile wouldn't have heard the door.

"Go in," Iona said to her sister.

"No, you go first."

"I'll go," Fannie Lou said, climbing down the steps and into the darkness that swallowed her whole. Leona didn't hesitate again; she simply climbed down into the darkness. Iona thought the woman gave the girl courage. She wished she could have some right about now. Instead, she took another good look at freedom before she followed her sister and this stranger into the belly of the whale. Inside, she couldn't see anything, not even the steps she trusted to be there when each foot reached out in front of the other. Somewhere below, her sister waited. The darkness was thick, and her eyes never seemed to get used to it. She reached the dirt floor and rubbed her foot across it, just to make sure.

To the right, she heard whispering, and she followed as best as she could, keeping her arms out so that she didn't bump into anything. Her hands touched a stone wall, and she followed it, feeling the cool stone as she moved. A stale breath flooded her face. "Leona?" she whispered, but the girl didn't say anything. A gust of stale air blew over her face, the smell rotten and foul. She wanted to scream, but getting caught scared her more than anything else. "Leona? Miss?" she called again, louder.

"Are you all right?" the woman finally answered. Her voice was across the room, many feet from Iona.

So Fannie Lou wasn't standing in front of her. But someone was still breathing on her; soft, steady, stale. It wasn't Leona, she knew. The person was too tall, his breath too deep. She slowly lifted her hand in front of her. Maybe she should just pretend that it wasn't there. She closed her eyes for a moment, her hand midair, and inhaled. When she opened her eyes, it was darker than it had been before. She decided to keep moving; maybe it would just go away.

Someone was standing before her, a cool face: eyes, nose, and open mouth brushed against her hand. She stopped, frozen, her hand still on the face. The cheeks underneath her hand moved as a smile spread wide within her fingers.

A light flickered, then ignited, and she saw Fannie Lou light a lantern hanging on the wall. The Negro face within her hand fluttered for a second before her and then faded away.

"Iona, come over here," the woman called. "Stay close. There's power here. Do you two feel it?" Neither of the girls answered.

Iona walked around the spot where the boy had stood, because she didn't want to feel any of the leftovers from him. When she got there, Fannie Lou held her hand back and forth over the bookshelf sitting in the corner. She stood like that for a long time until she finally found her prize and chose a small leather-bound book from the old, dusty bookshelf.

She pulled on the shelf and it slid open slowly, dust and dirt flying everywhere. Inside, there was a small room, not big enough to hold ten people standing toe to toe. It was dark.

"What is it?" Leona looked afraid.

"Don't know. Slave room, maybe. This may have been a stop on the Underground Slave Road. Hard to say. But there's something here, can't you feel it?"

Indeed the twins could feel it, tugging at their stomachs like a bass caught on the hook of a fishing line. "Is this what pulled us here?"

"It's always hard to tell at first. Sometimes it takes a while." Iona didn't know what the woman was talking about, and she was getting nervous in Mr. Fuller's basement. What if he caught them there?

Fannie Lou walked inside and kicked a pile of clothes lying in the middle of the stone floor. A large rat squalled, crawled out of the pile, and scurried into a hole in the wall. Another lantern hung on the wall, but she didn't light it.

"Yeah, as I suspected, these are old Negro clothes." She held the clothes to her nose and sniffed them. "And there's blood on 'em from back when we was here."

"When who was here? People blood?"

The woman nodded. "Think so." She paused for a minute and looked at each of the girls. "Think this is why we were drawn here. It's our past. Important."

Beside Iona, Leona grabbed her hand, squeezed. She thought for a second the girl was simply afraid of the dark, as they both had been for as long as Iona could remember. They each would wake the other up to go to the outhouse together at night, but mostly Leona held it until morning. Iona couldn't complain too much; she did the same thing—it was dark outside at night. Leona stiffened and moved closer to her sister, staring into the dark, abandoned room. Iona followed her gaze, and there in the middle of the rubble of clothes, in the middle of the room, something wiggled in the center of the pile. Then something shot straight up about an inch out of the pile. At first, Iona thought it was a worm, but then a second one appeared right beside it, and then a third and fourth. The four long, thin caterpillar things moved out of the ground, heavenward, as she realized they were attached to an arm. The little hand made its way through the clothing as a second set of four fingers appeared, pushing the pile to the side. A moment later, two tiny boney elbows arched from within the mound, the body still unseen. Somewhere in the bowels of the house, something stirred. The clothes rumbled.

All three stood and watched the young body emerge from within the rubble. Tiny hands, then arms, and then a small, black body. It appeared from seemingly nowhere, as the pile of clothes wasn't large enough to have hidden him.

Iona moaned a bit and turned her head. She always tried to pretend she couldn't see these things, but she saw this. She saw this. Her hand gripped Leona tighter, and she thought for sure she would bruise the girl. Iona turned to look at her sister; in this darkness, the only signs of her were her big, scared eyes and too-bright teeth.

As the trio watched, the dead figure climbed out of the clothes stack, like a spider from its hole, and crouched on the floor, staring at them. The boy was naked, maybe four years old. Blood streamed down the side of his face, and dirt covered his body so that his dark skin was almost invisible. He looked like he had been there for a long time. Dead. Perhaps buried in that shallow grave of dirty clothes, tossed away like unwanted trash.

He wobbled toward them on unsteady feet, as if he hadn't used them in a long time. And he in fact hadn't, Iona knew. He moved as if his legs hurt him somehow, as though one was shorter than the other. He slowly reached out to them, his fingers bloody and raw, his body worn and tired.

Iona slowly reached out her hand toward the boy. She didn't want to touch him, but she felt such sorrow. Her entire body ached for the pain that this child had suffered. She was only a young girl herself, but her mind flooded with images of large groups of people surrounded by men with whips and chains and guns. She closed her eyes, not wanting to see anymore, not wanting to *feel* or experience it any longer, but she could not block the images from her mind.

"Don't touch him. Take deep breaths," Fannie Lou urged. She walked over and placed a hand on each of the girls' shoulders. "It's overwhelming at first, but you have to keep calm and quiet as possible. If you scare the spook, the feeling gets ten times worse. They don't want to hurt you. They're scared themselves. They always are. Even if they're scary."

The woman reached into her pocket and pulled out a small cloth-wrapped bag. She opened the bag and pulled out a few grains of salt and herbs and sprinkled them along the floor. Then she spoke as if to no one, but with authority. "Suffer no more."

At first, Iona thought she was speaking to her because it was as if her pain completely vanished just as the words were spoken, but then the boy was gone, just as suddenly as he had appeared. The clothes were all back in a pile, as if they hadn't been moved at all.

The woman turned to look at them. "He's gone for now. But he can't leave without the others. That's what I'm come here to help you do."

"Now you know what I do. What you're meant to do." Fannie Lou stared at the girls, but they were simply glad to be out of the oppressive basement, and she wasn't sure that they understood the ramifications of what she said to them.

"What are we supposed to do?" Iona asked.

"Help them."

"How?"

"My dears, the land and elements and stars will all align for you in the right conditions, just for to help them. But, you must choose, quickly. Because they're coming for me and I have a lot to show you."

Iona shook her head. "I won't. I can't do things. I don't like it. It hurts people." She wrapped her tiny arms around herself and shook.

Leona took her sister's hand. "We have to go."

Fannie stared at them. "You don't have to run from this. It's who you are."

167

Without saying another word, the two girls ran away, disappeared through the trees. Fannie signed. They weren't ready.

10

Missus Davidson insisted that all the children, boys and girls alike, attend school at least one day a week so as to not forget their learnings, even though Missus Davidson said that boys were not quite as smart as girls were, and that they had to try harder just to get the same results. Iona didn't really know what the woman meant by "results"—none of the kids did, really—but she nodded her head and smiled, just to make the woman feel good. Anyway, she figured that Missus Davidson was probably making a wisecrack against the boys, and she was just fine with that. Especially Eddie Gray.

Missus Davidson had said that learning was the most important thing in the world and that it could take some people anywhere. She always looked at Leona when she said it, her eyes wide and bright—despite her own daughter, Sara, who sat only one seat away but was several full shades darker. She always said that *certain* folks had advantages that others didn't and that they should use it to get out of places like Colored Town, Kentucky. She always spit those words, *Colored Town, Kentucky,* like they stung her tongue. She was a heavyset woman, Missus Davidson. Momma always said she just had big bones, but if that were the case, then she had bigger bones than any women Iona had ever seen. She also had the biggest eyes. They kind of sat on her face, instead of *in* her face, like most people's. She was just about a shade darker than Leona, and she made sure no one forgot she was a worldly woman, as she called herself.

"I done seen me a good portion of the world, yes I have. I didn't have much trouble like some Negroes, neither. I used to be bright as Leona in my day. Not but a shade darker now, you see..." Then she'd go on about the things that most Negroes can't have and she had. Like getting into shows in New York City or fancy dances in California if she had the right man on her arm. She was a pretty woman, big or not, and Iona could tell that she had been beautiful once. She talked too much for a woman, though, Daddy said.

Every Monday, Iona and her sister got up extra early so they could make their way back to the church house and get their daily learning. It wasn't right; they had to spend all day in that church on

Sundays, just to come back again on Monday morning.

"Nobody should be forced to go to church two days in one week. God cain't hear but one prayer a week with all these people in the world prayin' an'ways," Iona whispered to her sister.

"But we ain't prayin'," Leona reminded her.

"I am. I'm prayin' for the day to be over soon."

By the time the girls got there the sun had come out and begun doing its best job of heating up the day like an oven. Most of the kids had already gotten there, and Missus Davidson was bending over some poor soul, helping him with his studies, her butt hitched up in the air, wiggling all around. She was wider than most people and took up most of the aisles when she walked down them.

They tried their best to come in without the woman noticing, but she saw them and smiled as they took their seats. She said she didn't show favorites, but Iona constantly reminded Leona that she was Missus Davidson's favorite. Leona claimed she didn't believe it, but you had to be blind not to notice. Leona wasn't blind.

Eddie Gray came into the church late, as usual. Missus Davidson looked at him and sighed. "Where you been, Eddie Gray?" She always said his name like that, the first and last name together. It was kind of threatening, the way she said it. If Leona was her favorite, then Eddie Gray was, by far, her most hated child in class. You could see it in her eyes, through the worn crow's feet and all.

Eddie Gray shrugged his shoulders, as if he didn't even care to answer her. Most of the time he didn't, anyway. Most of the time Missus Davidson would send him away or talk to his momma on Sundays when she was there. It didn't usually matter; Eddie Gray would always be the same. Daddy said it was because he didn't have no daddy.

"What was that?" Missus Davidson bent down in front of his face. She would probably skin the tar off of him. She kept a thick wooden paddle with big circles carved into it in a drawer somewhere behind the altar. She called it her "peace stick," and usually when she used it there was anything but peace in that room. She mainly used it to threaten children, and usually it worked: with just seeing it, a kid would behave. But not Eddie Gray. She had busted his butt with it so many times, Iona had lost count.

"Don't know," Eddie finally said.

"Get up, Eddie Gray." The boy stood, and she dragged him by

his arm over to the corner. For the life of her, Leona didn't know why the boy still came to school. Maybe his momma made him. There weren't many boys who kept up with schooling after they were ten years old or so, and Eddie was already twelve. He worked in the fields all the time; Leona had seen him. Maybe, she supposed, he really wanted to learn.

Eddie Gray said something nasty to Missus Davidson, and she whacked him upside the head.

Maybe not.

The heat was so bad inside the church during school sometimes that some of the boys had taken to wearing no shirts and only cut-off britches during the summers. But Missus Davidson would have none of that. She said she could just as well whoop bare backs and legs, and it would sting twice as bad. The boys stopped it real quick after that.

They sat in that room, learning only how it felt to roast like a pig on a stick. Missus Davidson had a pretty little handkerchief that she kept blotting her head with until she had to wring the thing out in a bucket in the corner. Iona knew it wasn't right, but she smiled a bit, knowing that the woman was uncomfortable. She looked over at Leona and found that her sister was enjoying it too.

Outside the window, something popped against it, rattling the pane. Everyone turned to look, but there was nothing there. As everyone was getting back to their lessons—six times six was thirty-six or thirty-seven, Iona wasn't sure—something else hit the windowpane. A long, thin crack split the glass. Several kids jumped to their feet, looking out. A succession of bees swarmed over their heads, and they realized that the noises had not come from outside, but had been the bees trying to get back out through the glass.

One of the girls yelled out. Everyone started screaming and jumping around, which seemed to agitate the bees that much worse. They darted for the kids. Missus Davidson tried to get everyone to calm down, but one of the bees caught her in the cheek and she screamed louder than everyone else, her bass-filled voice sounding very strange in that small room.

Above their heads, a large beehive peeked out from behind one of the rafters. Iona hadn't noticed it before, and now it seemed thousands of bees swarmed from the pulsing hive. For a brief moment, Iona wondered where it had come from. Mr. James, who was as old as sin itself and as mean as a bobcat, cleaned out the church once a month real good, ensuring there wasn't any dirt hiding in the corners. Sometimes he would be at it all night, making the place spotless. Mr. James only had one good eye and his back wasn't straight anymore, but he would work himself until he was dead, he had assured them all. Iona was sure that he would have gotten that beehive out of that church, or he would have died trying.

As the bees swarmed around her head, one landing on her ear just before she batted it away, she thought there was a strangeness about the bees. But she didn't know what it was.

Several of the kids got stung trying to run out as the little monsters did their best to do the same. Something poked Iona in the back, and she thought for sure she had been stung, but when she looked, Leona was holding her, trying to get her under the pew. She fell to the floor as a particularly vicious-looking bee dove toward her head. Just as it passed, she and her sister jumped to their feet and ran toward the door. But before they reached it, a giant swarm twirled through the air toward them. Both girls watched, frozen in place, seemingly entranced by the colony of vicious creatures.

Outside, in the hot, humid air, a voice screamed at the girls to run. Their teacher waved her thick arms back and forth, signaling the girls to get out of the church. Neither Leona nor Iona moved; they felt compelled to watch, as if something was keeping them bolted in their spots. Suddenly, the bees dove toward them. A dark wave of spiraling mass collided with the girls, completely encasing them within its midst. For a moment, everything was completely quiet. Nothing moved. Nothing stirred. To the girls, even the thunderous buzzing sound was muted, and calm overtook them.

Simultaneously, the girls remembered Fannie's voice: *the land and elements and stars will all align for you in the right conditions.* Were the bees trying to protect them? Neither of the girls could explain it, but they felt connected to the swarm. They could feel its pulse drumming through them, as if they all were one: Leona, Iona, and the mass of honeybees.

The girls gathered their senses, realizing that they felt more connected to the world than they ever had in their lives. Outside, people had begun to gather around as Missus Davidson sent the children to get help. Slowly, deliberately, the twins walked outside together, hand in hand. As the twins emerged from the building, the bees covering them like a shield, a carpet of pulsing, throbbing mass, the people of town collectively gasped.

Most only watched, fearful, but several shooed at the mass, getting stung themselves in the process.

"Water," someone yelled. "Get a bucket of water."

"No. They'll hurt the girls," someone else countered.

Just then, Fannie Lou appeared. She stood in front of Leona and Iona, taking each of the girls' free hands. As she clung to them, the bees began to spread up her hand, then her arm, until they had consumed her entire body, too. The three stood there, as if in a frozen dance together.

After what felt like forever, Fannie whispered several words, released the girls, and raised her hands to the sky. Seemingly instantaneously, the bees became agitated again, fluttering their wings. The crowd jumped and moved away. Then the bees were gone. Just like that. They flew away, back where they had come from, leaving no trace of ever having been there at all.

The girls and woman stood as the crowd of people stared at them.

Before Fannie could say anything, Leona's and Iona's father grabbed the girls and pulled them away from the woman, as if she was a danger to them.

Finally, Fannie Lou walked in the other direction. The whispers grew louder as she walked.

They couldn't wait any longer. The twins sneaked out of the house and went to Fannie Lou that night. They knew they should have gone to her before then, but the truth was that they were scared. The woman herself didn't scare them, but the things she had told them did. They believed Fannie. Each of the girls could feel the power within herself growing strong until it felt as if it would consume her. Likewise, the link that the pair shared seemed to tighten, wound thicker between them until it felt like an unbreakable wire that connected them to each other.

When they arrived at the Warren's door, Fannie was waiting. Finally, Leona spoke, but she did not make eye contact. "How are we supposed to help people? You said we were meant...that things would align for us. How do you mean?" She looked sideways at her sister, as if asking on her behalf.

Fannie smiled. "You've felt it? With the bees, right?"

The girls nodded.

"And other things, maybe?"

Neither girl answered, until Leona blurted out, "You mean help dead people, don't you?" The girl didn't really like this whole idea, Fannie Lou knew. But Iona seemed different; she relished it. Iona was a lot like Fannie Lou; her powers made her feel special in a way that the cruel world never had. Fannie understood that.

"I mean people that are trapped here because of no fault of their own and we have to help. And you have to learn how to control those powers of yours."

Leona was much more willing to make eye contact now. "Where are you from? You talk funny and you act like...like, I don't know. Like you not scared of nothing."

Fannie Lou looked at Leona, then Iona, and smiled. "I can't say I have a home. I search for...people like you that can make things a little better. I'm drawn to them, like you were to that basement. Like you are to each other. Do you understand?"

"No!" Leona yelled.

Fannie sighed. "I came here to teach you how to...cleanse. I want to help you use your God-given powers."

Leona snorted. "Powers. You're a witch, aren't you?"

"No more than you are."

Leona flinched as if hit. Fannie stopped, slowed down. She didn't want to scare them or lose them to their fear. "Listen, very few people are capable of doing the things that we—" She made a circle with her fingers, pointing to each one of them, including herself. "—can do. And most of those people throughout history have been women. That scares people. If it had been restricted to men, then it'd be revered. But because it's the power of women, they call us witches, or Hoodoo women, or Rootworkers, or a whole host of other things. There was a time when we were valued; not anymore. But it's important that you learn how to harness this power. There are so few of us left."

"What are we?" Iona had been quiet up until then.

Fannie decided to answer her honestly. "I don't know. It's in our heritage, the blood of our ancestors. I was sought out and found and taught the same way I found you and the way I hope you, one day, you will find others. We're nomads; can't stay in one place for too long before we're called—pulled—to another. Or we're run out. That's just how it is." She hung her head, ashamed for subjecting these girls to what she knew was a hard life. But if she didn't, they might never understand and always feel as if they were missing something, or feel as if there was something that they should be doing. This was better, she knew, but that didn't make it any easier.

"Are there more of us?" Iona knew the right questions to ask. She would be long for this journey.

"Yes. Some are not so good. Some...collect instead of teach, and that's why I'm here. You need to understand what you can do, and what could happen. There are people—powerful beings—that may come—"

"For us?"

Fannie nodded. "One day, maybe. But I'll do what I can. Teach you what I know before I have to move on."

"Move on?" Leona seemed to be coming around.

"You heard your minister. I can't be trusted. I'm a witch."

She looked at the girls and knew their lives would change from this moment on. There were places and people they would see that they could not have imagined only a day before. They were different; she hoped they understood this.

"Let's get started. Control is the key..."

11

He chased her from the schoolhouse through the woods, mocking her as Missus Davidson had mocked him only days before. Iona had known that Eddie Gray wouldn't leave her alone, and she had been right. He had caught her after school alone and had told her he was going to make her pay.

She just needed to be by herself—so many things had happened. Leona had understood how she felt and had walked home without her—she had done the same for her sister in the past. Iona just needed to think about the things that Fannie Lou had told them. She wasn't sure she wanted this; using her powers had only caused Widow Robinson pain. Why bother anymore?

That was when Eddie Gray had found her, alone. She had taken off running for her house, dodging in and out of the trees, trying to get away. Everything seemed so far, far beyond her reach and now she didn't think she'd make it. Her house was a long way away, and her legs were hurting. Behind her, the boy laughed and called out her name. She didn't think he'd hit her, but she didn't want to take any chances. Eddie was scared of her brothers, all of them. But her brothers weren't around right now.

"Where's that witch to help you now?" he said. "I don't see 'er. And I don't care if you tell. I'm gonna whoop your ass good." He was getting tired; she could hear it in his voice. She thought maybe if she could just outrun him, things would be fine. If she could just get beyond the tree line, and into the field...

Now that she thought about it, she didn't like that idea at all. The only reason she had been able to stay away from him for this long was because they had been running in the woods and she could maneuver through the trees well because she was so little. If they got out into the open, he would catch her for sure. His legs were long and much stronger than hers.

She decided to change direction. She headed south, and just as she turned, Eddie reached out, grabbing her dress. She ducked around a tree and ripped away from him, tearing a hole in the fabric. Her momma was going to kill her for messing up her dress. She had made a pair special for the girls and had been proud when she surprised them with the dresses only weeks before.

In the distance she saw the shack; it seemed to call to her. It stood quiet, its paint faded with age and decay. Vines and moss covered much of the house, except the doorway. It stood as an open black hole. There was no light beyond, almost like a vacuum. But this was a welcome sight to her. She picked up her pace, hoping to get into the house before he could follow.

She reached the tree just in front of the door and stopped, out of breath, and looked back. Eddie Gray was closer than she'd thought; he would certainly see that she had entered the house. She dashed up the rickety old stairs and into the house. She stopped just for a second, searching the building she knew all too well. She ran to the closet door, threw it open, and stepped into the pile of moldy shoes and shut the door, just as she heard the boy reach the top stair.

Outside the door, the house creaked and moaned like an old woman, and Eddie's footfalls came closer to the closet door. Then they stopped. Walked away, toward the back of the house. After several seconds, they returned and walked toward the stairway.

"Where are you, Iona? Are you up there?"

Beneath her, the shoes began to move and sway under her sandaled feet. She looked down, but it was too black. The shoelaces began wiggling and crawling around, like live worms. They clawed at her tiny toes, slimy and moist and smelling like dead earth. She wanted to scream, but she covered her mouth with both hands, yelling between her numb fingers. Several of the tendrils wiggled their way up her legs, toward her knees. She could feel the slippery laces pulling the old, unused shoes behind them like dead weight. She could only imagine the sight of these worm-like things attached to the shoes, dragging them around like newborn babies and their umbilical cords. Was this what they did when no one was around to see it? She wasn't sure she wanted to know.

In the house, Eddie worked his way up the stairs. Her hand still covering her mouth, she couldn't bring herself to stop him from going up there. She and her sister had been playing in that house for as long as she could remember. In fact, her brothers had been the ones to show them the shack and its mysterious room of shoes. But as far as she knew, none of them had ever gone up the steps. It was too scary up there, too dark, as if light was not permitted to enter that space. As if the living weren't either.

Eddie screamed.

For a second, Iona thought he was faking, trying to get her to come out. She wasn't going to fall for it; no way. He screamed again, loud, and she knew he wasn't faking. Above her head, something tumbled to the floor, rattling the boards, knocking dust into her eyes. Eddie called out again, but this time it was louder, more terrifying.

She dashed out of the closet and got to the stairs just as something pulled Eddie, head first, into the back of the house. "Iona! Iona, help me—" he screamed. She ran up the steps, but stopped short of the top step. She had never been this far up before. She couldn't see anything beyond where she stood. It was completely quiet. Nothing moved. She looked down at the stairs, wanting to go up, do whatever she could to help the boy, but she couldn't.

The truth was she didn't like Eddie. Her heart pounded in her chest, aching for him, but she didn't want to go up there to help him. Not him. Not Eddie. Iona's stomach turned, and she almost threw up her oatmeal breakfast. It would probably be the same texture coming out as it had been going in.

Iona had never contemplated physically helping someone. She didn't know if she even could. If she was strong enough. After all, she had spent all of her short years making people feel better about themselves. She just had a way of making people okay again, making them whole. Perhaps she hadn't been able to do this for Eddie the same way she hadn't for the widow. Or perhaps, deep down, she hadn't wanted to. Maybe she had never thought he was worth it.

At that moment, something flew from the back of the house, where Eddie Gray had been dragged, straight past her head. She had to duck as a second identical shoe almost hit her in the head. As she watched, each of the shoes that had been on Eddie's feet only moments before bounced down the stairs. Just as they did in the twin's game. They reached the bottom of the steps and stopped, as if staring at her, the strings wiggling like worms.

That was it; she couldn't take it anymore. She thought about all the things the boy had said and done to her, and she began to feel resentment toward him. Perhaps Fannie Lou had gotten under her skin—the woman was so strong-willed. Iona respected her, she wanted to be just like her. She didn't want to be a victim to Eddie Gray anymore.

My dears, the land and elements will align...to help you.

Iona ran out of the house, not stopping, not looking back. And not bothering to help the boy.

Not Eddie. Not that day.

12

Jesus wept.

He wept for humanity in the Holy Bible, and He wept for the people of Colored Town on the evening they decided they could no longer stand Ms. Fannie Lou Mason within their town limits. They claimed it was the missing Gray boy that pushed them over the edge, but the truth was, the bees had scared them. Most people in town didn't particularly care for Eddie Gray one way or another—he was a bad seed, they said—but he made for a nice excuse against the Hoodoo woman trying to harm the young children in town.

There was something about the sound of horses galloping on compacted dirt that filled Fannie Lou with dread. She had experienced them in every town and parish that she had ever visited. The sound always seem to preface something bad, something she usually couldn't stop or control.

It was the word "witch." It would do it every time. Reasonable, sensible people could completely lose their minds as long as they believed that there was a woman of little moral character involved—a woman who cavorted with evil. Those people were usually upstanding members of their community, and it never mattered what they were, or where they came from—fear was fear.

In every single one of those towns a small part of her died. They had murdered her.

Several men banged on the Warrens' door. Mr. Warren rose to his feet, and his wife walked over and wrapped her arm around her husband. Fannie Lou's heart raced. She was scared, but mostly for the Warrens; she didn't want anything to happen to them.

"They're here for me." She walked toward the door.

"Wait. Let me talk to them. I know these men. I can reason with 'em. Send 'em back home."

She didn't want him to do this. It would put him in danger, and she didn't think he understood the situation fully. Mr. Warren might know *these* men, but she knew *all* men. She reached into her bag, tore off a chunk of herb, and popped it into her mouth, under her tongue.

Before she could stop him, Mr. Warren opened the door. The preacher stood in the doorway. He was dressed in his Sunday best, although this was Wednesday night. He clutched a Bible in his hands, the gold holy lettering spilling over the edges of his fingers. He looked afraid.

"Evening, gentlemen. Help ya?" Mr. Warren asked.

Behind the preacher who didn't have a name—or at least whose name Fannie Lou didn't know—several people watched. Including Mr. Pace. There were about thirty of them in all, both men and women. Most she recognized from church or from around town.

"We just want to talk to her." The preacher pointed at Fannie. She didn't say anything. She had learned long ago that it was the best way.

Mr. Warren looked back at her as if he was surprised. "Fannie Lou? What you want her for? It's late."

"You know quite well what, Warren. Don't be pretending you

don't know what she claim to be."

Warren shot him a look. "I ain't heard her claim nothin'. I done heard you claimin' things you don't know nothin' about. Now why don't you all go home and forget this nonsense?"

"Old man, you have no idea. You think I don't know that you help her? You think we're all blind?"

What in the hell was he talking about? Fannie Lou wasn't sure, but she didn't like where this was going. Since Fannie had arrived in town, she hadn't spent much time in the house. But why did this matter? What was the point?

"What are you talkin' about?" Mr. Warren asked.

"Sinful, lustful souls shall be damned," the preacher said. "No hidin', no more pretendin'."

That was it, then. She was not only a witch, a Hoodoo Woman, but a whore, too. She would corrupt the souls of men, using her body. Heaven help her. What happened to the good old days of just being the devil's ally? She stared at the preacher. He, in turn, continued to look down on Mr. Warren, as he stood a full foot taller.

Mr. Warren shook his head. "You lyin' sack a'—"

Fannie interrupted him, against her better judgment. She didn't want him to say anything that he would regret; he had to live here with these people, even after she was gone. "The Warrens have been very gracious to open their doors to me. But I don't want to cause any trouble for them or for myself."

Mr. Pace snorted from behind the preacher. "Too late."

The preacher held up his hand, quieting the man. "What have you done with Eddie Gray?"

"Who is Eddie Gray?" Fannie knew very well who Eddie Gray was; she had threatened the boy not long ago. But she thought it best to not mention that.

The man stared at her. She stared back, eye to eye. No matter what, she would not let this holy man intimidate her. She had seen many men like him, and she would see many more. As he watched her, he became more and more uncomfortable. Fannie knew that people who found themselves staring into her eyes saw a reflection of their true selves within her gaze. Most people could not handle the truth. This preacher was no different.

After a moment, the man looked away. Sometimes...sometimes

this would be enough to send them on their way. Not this man.

"We know you did something. Someone saw you talking to him outside of the church, with the Kelly twin. We will not let you have him, you Hoodoo bitch."

So much for subtleties. *Damn*, she needed more time.

She had spent the last few weeks with the twins, teaching them everything she could about who they were. But it wasn't enough; she needed more time. Each of the girls was different, and she realized that they worked together, as a unit. This made them quite power- ful, indeed. She had told them that they needed to keep it all a se- cret, even from their parents. As she looked into the crowd, she was glad for that.

Pace stormed into the house. Mr. Warren tried to stop him, but he pushed the old man aside. Mrs. Warren stood in front of Fannie, blocking the man. Fannie was glad that she had not believed what the preacher had said about her and the woman's husband, but she could not let anything happen to this family. She placed her hand on the woman's shoulder.

"It's okay."

Mrs. Warren shook her head and looked at the preacher. "You come into my house. Attack my guest. Don't do this. Please."

"Get out of the way. We're saving your soul."

Fannie kissed the woman on the cheek and walked outside, into the crowd.

"Where is my son?" a woman yelled. *She must be Eddie's mother*, thought Fannie. The woman looked upset and angry. She had tears in her eyes, but they were tears of rage, not worry. She really believed that the Fannie had done something to her son.

"Listen, people—" Fannie tried to reason with them, but the preacher stopped her.

"Don't try to vex us all with lies. Where is the boy?"

"I never laid a hand on that child." Her tongue was beginning to feel numb from the herbs in her mouth.

The mother ran up and slapped her. Fannie didn't have time to react or protect herself. She should have expected it because the woman was so angry, but she still hoped she could get control of the situation. Now that the first blow had been struck, that was probably not going to happen.

The woman reached out to strike her again, but before she

could, another man came from within the crowd and punched Fannie in the stomach. She fell to her knees, holding her stomach. The pain vibrated from her belly throughout her body, and she almost swallowed the contents of her mouth. The man rose to kick her, and Fannie reacted quickly. She spit toward the man, creating a barrier between him and herself. Just as his foot would have connected with her body, a spark of electricity threw him backward, off his feet.

The crowd gasped. "See, I told you," the preacher yelled. "She has to die."

"Stop this, Joseph." A man walked up and stood between Fannie and the preacher. *Preacher Joseph*, Fannie thought bitterly.

"What are you doing here, Walter? Shouldn't you be at home with those girls?" Behind the newcomer, the twins stood watching her. Fannie realized that this was their father; she recognized him from the church.

"I'm here to stop you from doing something stupid. Jesus, Joseph, what are you doing? This ain't right. You know it ain't."

The preacher shook his finger at Fannie. "She comes here to hurt us, and if we let her, she will destroy our town. She'll poison us, make us turn against each other. That's what they do. We worked so hard to build this. You know what we have to do."

The twins watched, neither knowing what to say. They both looked so small standing there, so unprepared. Fannie wondered briefly if they were ready, but quickly put the thought out of her head. Both girls had kept their secret about the time that the three had spent together. She knew they wanted to tell, because they believed it was wrong to keep secrets, but she had warned them against it. She had told them some of the things that could happen if people found out. They had obviously listened. Although that didn't exactly mean they were ready, it did show that the girls understood the consequences of their gifts.

"I saw her," someone shouted. "I saw her lead the boy into the woods." It was obviously a lie, but she would bet that the woman who said it actually believed that she had seen what she said—or at least she thought it was the right thing to say.

Before Fannie could defend herself, a rock flew through the air and hit her in the head. She grunted and bent over in pain. Blood spilled down her face, into her eye. Several more rocks flew through the air, hitting her over and over again. At first she tried to dodge them, but they began coming so rapidly she couldn't get away from them. She spit into the air to block them, but her mixture was so diluted by blood it was ineffective. She tried to rise to her feet, but her legs and feet were numb, and she tumbled back to the ground.

The twins' father held the girls in his arms, protecting his daughters, while the girls fought to get to her. No doubt the man understood that at any moment the crowd could turn on the girls. After all, most of the town knew and had seen what had happened with the girls and the bees. That would be enough to condemn them. Perhaps her blood would be enough to slake their lust.

A large woman pushed through the crowd, screaming. Everyone stopped and looked at the girl, her belly bigger than her head. Janice got on her knees in front of Fannie and used her thick, swollen hands to brush some of the blood out of the woman's eyes. But the blood was too thick, and there was too much of it. The girl began to use her own dress to sop up the liquid and dress the wounds. Fannie touched the girl's hands, weakly. Without warning, a large man ran from within the crowd and grabbed the girl. She screamed and fought him, but he slapped her. Stunned, Janice fell backward and the man wrapped his arms around her waist and carried her away. The pair disappeared into the horde of people.

Everyone was silent for a moment. What went on inside people's homes was their own business. But to make it public was another matter altogether. Their only dilemma, Fannie knew, was her. God gave explicit instructions on what to do under threat of a witch, but his directions became much less clear when discussing matters of men's reign over women.

Just then someone made a decision: a particularly large rock flew at Fannie. As the mini-boulder flew through the sky toward the woman, the youngest twin, Iona, wrestled away from her father and ran to protect her. The rock hit the girl, piercing her back, knocking her off her feet. The small arsenal continued to soar and Fannie tried to cover Iona with her own body. One after another, the rocks sliced open the woman's flesh, spilling her blood.

As her vision began to fade, Fannie heard the twins' father hollering, trying to get the crowd under control. He ran up to one of the men and knocked him to the ground, then he tackled another. Finally, several more people tried to help him get the others to stop.

Underneath Fannie, the girl groaned. Fannie tried to ask Iona if she was all right, but she was losing consciousness and couldn't clear her head. She could hear labored breathing and felt that there was something not quite right with the girl. The rocks stopped after what seemed like an incredibly long time, and she sat up to give Iona breathing room.

"Iona!" the girl's twin screamed. A bloom of blood flowered on Iona's shirt, slowly spreading like a wild red rose. Leona dropped to her knees beside her sister as their mother and father gathered around them. Fannie gathered her strength and ripped open the girl's shirt. Despite her best effort, several sharp rocks had stricken the girl. One of them had put a hole in the girl's temple.

Fannie touched the girl, connecting to her as she had in the woods only a few weeks before. Iona's chest was heavy and she breathed hard, taking long, slow breaths to try to get air into her lungs. But it was difficult. Fannie was weak, herself, and she couldn't feel the girl as well as she should have. Instead, Iona seemed lost. She was fading.

"I...I..." Fannie slowly opened her eyes and tried to speak but couldn't get the words out.

A white light appeared in the distance, and Fannie watched as it brightened its way toward the girl. It was her time.

"No, damn it. You cannot fucking have her." Fannie was aware that people were watching her, but she didn't care. Tears streamed down her face and she shook the girl to ensure she didn't fade away.

Iona opened her eyes. "Why are you crying, Ma'am?"

Fannie coughed, and blood covered her hands when she removed them from her mouth. Fannie looked down, smiling at the girl. "They're not taking you. I mean it."

"It's okay."

Leona shook her head, crying. "No. No. No."

"Am I dying?" Iona asked.

"Yes."

Leona and her mother burst into tears as they watched the two. Mrs. Kelly knelt at her daughter's feet. Her husband stood behind her, silent.

What in the hell had she done? She had come here, as she had in many different towns, but she had not planned for this to happen. She was supposed to protect the girls, not condemn them.

Fannie Lou raised her head to the sky. The night was particularly quiet, as most of the anger had shot right out of people as they saw what they had done to the little girl. She closed her eyes, breathing in the fresh Kentucky air. She tried as much as she could to clear her mind. It was still foggy, and she knew there was something very wrong with her own body, but that didn't matter right now. She spoke to Mr. and Mrs. Kelly, ignoring everything else. "Your daughter will not die tonight. Not if I can help it. Not this little girl, damn it."

"Leona," Fannie said, "run into the house and get my bag. Go girl. Now!" Leona jumped to her feet and ran into the house. She was gone what seemed like an extremely long time, and Fannie could feel Iona fading away with each moment. Finally, Leona flew out of the house carrying a handmade bag that seemed heavy on her shoulders. Fannie knew how difficult it was to carry the contents of the bag. It only looked small to the untrained eye.

She took it from the girl and opened it. "We have work to do. Are you ready?"

Leona nodded, but looked frightened.

"Will you stay with me?"

"Yes."

The girl touched Fannie, felt her. "You're not going to make it."

"We have to hurry. Only you two are important now. You understand? Take her hand."

Leona hesitated for a moment in fear. Iona's skin had become as pale as her sister's as the pain ate at her from the inside out. Fannie Lou grabbed Iona's face. "You can let it go. Life wants you. You have so many things to do. So, so many things..." Fannie closed her eyes for a moment and almost passed out, but she knew that if she did, she wouldn't wake up again.

Fannie Lou held on, just a bit longer, and reached for Leona. "Help me heal your sister." The girl shook her head, unsure. She understood that Leona was scared, but she needed her now. "I'm not strong enough to do it on my own. "

The girl looked confused. "I cain't. I don't know how. I just cain't."

"You can. Just give her a part of yourself."

Leona grabbed her hand, squeezed tightly, and got on her knees over Iona's head, placing her small, pale hands on her sister's cheeks. A surge of energy passed through the group, from Leona to Fannie to Iona. The black girl's body jumped as if shocked. Fannie's fingers caressed Iona's hand, shaking and trembling from the power. A bright light exploded from the three—brighter than any sun—lighting the night sky.

Iona's body convulsed so badly her father almost pulled her away.

His wife stopped him. "Wait. They'll help her."

"She could die."

"She's already dying," the woman said simply.

The light grew brighter, and most people covered their eyes. It was too bright, some whispered, how could they stand it? The three lit up the sky so brightly that folks from miles around watched from porches, fields and barns, staring at the unexplained light from Colored Town.

Finally, it just died out, like a candle burning down to its base. Leona stood for a moment, looking around, unsure of what to do next. Fannie Lou smiled, the hole in her head bleeding so badly now she was surrounded by a pool of her own blood.

But Iona was healed. She opened her eyes, and they were as bright and as full of life as they had ever been. The wound in her head had completely closed up, the fluids seeming to flow from no source. She sat up and touched her sister. Her mother screamed, but it was from relief. Her father showed no emotion at all.

Fannie Lou Mason finally closed her eyes. She followed the light meant for Iona into nowhere.

13

The twins waited on the bank of Muller's creek for their job. The sun was just setting, the sky that perfect milky cream color, and things seemed like they would be this way forever.

That was when they saw them, in the distance. Ratty clothes hanging from too-thin bodies, shoes worn into nothing but soles and straps, and eyes as dead as they had been when they were alive. As Fannie Lou had told them, the old Negroes wandered the night, searching for a place they would never find. A place they had been seeking for God knew how long.

The girls figured that the dead Negroes had been there a very long time, although the twins hadn't really seen them before, only kind of felt their presence. But they had never manifested this way. Fannie Lou had taught them what to do and how to send them to the beyond, just as they had done for her only a few days earlier. The dead were roaming the woods, searching for their way, and only Leona and Iona could get them there.

You have to do it together now. You work better that way, as one, together, Fannie Lou had told them.

This made them proud, they had to admit. They liked the idea of being the only people able to help someone else. They liked helping people; they liked the feeling it gave them, the way they felt after they had done it. They also liked knowing they needed to do it together. They had always known they worked better together, as if they were one.

The dead men, women, and children—one of them the boy they had seen climb out of the clothes in Mr. Fuller's basement room—moved toward the girls as if they didn't see them. They did, the girls knew. They, however, had assumed that the girls couldn't see them. Most ghosts assumed this, Fannie had said. The dead stopped after a moment, the man in front gasping on air that he would never need again. Someone had been chasing them through the trees. Behind them, a group of armed white men ran and screamed. The group would not make it; the twins could see the anguish in the people's faces.

There were six white men. Each one carried a gun and wore a great big sun hat to protect him for the Indian summer, as they called it.

"Stop, damn it!" one of them yelled.

The Negroes turned around, tired of running. They stared at the white men. Neither of the girls had ever seen such contempt in a man's face as that Negro had that day. The black man charged the white one, as the group of Negroes behind him followed. The white men didn't hesitate; they raised their guns and fired.

Death soared though the sky right at the Negroes, but they didn't stop. They wanted to die, the girls knew. They wanted it all over.

Leona and Iona stepped in between the Negro group and the white men's bullets, and each girl held out a hand, unseen power circling them, absorbing everything around them. The trees moved without sign of a breeze in the sky and the ground trembled as a bright light swirled around them.

The Negro man looked at them. "What did you do, girl? Is this some kinda witches' doin'?"

The girls said in unison, as if they were one, "No."

They didn't know if it was true, but it sounded like the right thing to say. They carried Momma's Bible with them, each holding onto it while it was between them. Fannie Lou had said that they didn't need it, but hers had always made her feel better, and they had to agree it was comforting. It made them feel like Fannie Lou was right there with them, helping them, guiding them.

"What you want?"

"We want to help you get to where you're goin'."

The man in front shook his wobbly head. He hadn't eaten in days before they had died, wanting to save enough for the women and children. The girls could see everything they had gone through. It had broken the man, body and mind. "We ain't goin' nowhere but here, girl. Ain't got no choice."

"We can help you."

"They don't want us no mo'. We cain't get home." He had done this for so long.

"It takes everyone. Our friend told us that." Leona looked at her sister; the girl returned her smile.

The man looked back at the bullets stopped in midair. "What 'bout those who come after us? They have to know. We have to show 'em. Who gonna tell 'em? You?"

The girls didn't know what to say. Did things get better before you finally died and went to heaven? It hadn't for Fannie Lou.

"We cain't go. They have to know. They have ta'."

"We'll tell 'em. We promise."

The man nodded and looked to the people behind him, who he had guided for so long. "We goin' home now. We goin' home."

Leona and Iona held the Bible between them and directed the group toward them. Leona touched her baby sister's fingers, caressing them as much as she could across the black cover of the heavy, reassuring weight of the book.

The man who had been talking stayed back, letting the others go before him. The woman with the baby walked up to the girls and seemingly merged with them, as if through an invisible wall. A slight wind blew over the girls as they were engulfed by the scent of earth and breast milk—the woman's and her baby's scents, they knew. The Bible shook between their hands from the power, but the girls held firm.

One by one, the people passed through the girls and into the place they had been longing to see since well before Leona and Iona had been born. Such an odd thing, the girls knew, that these people had passed before them, but could not get home without them. A bright light died as each of them passed, and the girls realized that it was the soul of the person who had just left this earth for someplace else. Neither girl pretended to know where that place was. The book trembled with each one, as if accepting the soul itself within its pages.

Finally, it was the last man's turn. He had waited patiently while the others were delivered, watching and smiling as the others moved on. He walked up to the girls but did not enter.

"You promise?"

The girls nodded. "We promise."

Then, he, like the others, merged with them, his body becoming part of them, his smell engulfing their noses.

This was the first of many times that the girls would cleanse together. Fannie Lou had been right; they needed one another to help others. They were each driven by the promise they had made that day in the woods to a dead man.

And by the woman, Fannie Lou Mason.

Acknowledgements

First, I would like to thank my family, who are always there for me, even when I screw up—and because I do it so often, your jobs are terribly difficult. These are, in no certain order: Silas, Jete', Brooke, Essence, Trinity, Annie Mae, Carlanda, Chaka and Chadvina. This is for you!

Others who have made this possible in one way or another: Maurice Broaddus, my annoying inner conscience; Sara Larson, the most awesome lady; Tyhitia Green, my friend; Shannan Palma, one of the smartest women I know; Lawana Holland-Moore, who is always there for me; Monica Gresham, for the late night phone calls; Charlotte Kubicz, my French connection; William (Bill) Lynch, the electricity guy; Emily Wagner, the human rolodex, and Neil Simpkins from Agnes Scott College.

Finally, I'd like to thank Jason Sizemore for taking a chance on the angry, big-mouth, black chick in the genre and Deb Taber, my delightful editor.

Thank you all so much.

Artist Biography

A native of Denver, Colorado, Jordan Casteel is an artist and a graduate of Agnes Scott College where she earned a BA in Studio Arts. In addition, Ms. Casteel has studied at the University of Georgia John Kehoe School of the Arts in Cortona, Italy. Ms. Casteel's works have been exhibited in both Denver, Colorado in "Yansan: 100 Year of Womyn's Struggle, Ceremony and Sword" and in Atlanta, Georgia in "CIAO: I Direttori." Several of her works are owned in private collections.

For Ms. Casteel, identities are not static, but always shifting. She is in a constant search for beauty that she believes exists in every soul. Her ideology is rooted in a passion for identity politics. Particularly through the use of oil paint and large canvases, she has created spaces in which people can be represented authentically. She makes art because she believes life is about building meaningful relationships with those around her, and it has given her an opportunity to explore those relationships—through color, form and composition. Color and skin tones are often associated as specifically being shades of brown, but she sees so much more than that. She sees human faces as a mosaic of colors that represent the layers of our existence.

For more information about Jordan Casteel visit her website at www.jordancasteel.com.

Author Biography

Chesya Burke has published over forty short stories in various venues including *Dark Dreams: Horror and Suspense by Black Writers, Voices From the Other Side,* and *Whispers in the Night,* each published by Kensington Publishing Corp. as well as the historical, science, and speculative fiction magazine, *Would That It Were,* and many more. Several of her articles appeared in the *African American National Biography,* published by Harvard and Oxford University Press, and she won the 2004 Twilight Tales award for short fiction. Chesya attends Agnes Scott College, where she studies creative writing and the African diaspora as it relates to race, class and gender. Many of these themes find themselves appearing in her fiction.

Visit her at www.chesyaburke.com or on her blog (chesyaburke.livejournal.com), where she tends to discuss these issues and genre fiction as well.

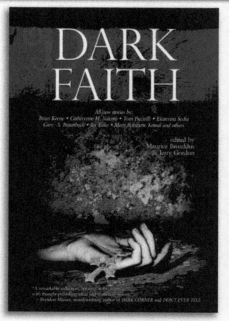